WEALTHEOW

HER TELLING OF BEOWULF

WEALTHEOW

HER TELLING OF BEOWULF

ASHLEY CROWNOVER

Wealtheow: Her Telling of Beowulf

Library of Congress Cataloging-in-Publication Data

Crownover, Ashley.
  Wealtheow : her telling of Beowulf / Ashley Crownover.
    p. cm.
ISBN 978-1-59652-390-6 (hc) -- ISBN 978-1-59652-391-3 (pbk.)
I. Title.
 PS3603.R76W43 2008
813'.6 -- dc22

                        2007052321

Iroquois Press
An imprint of Turner Publishing Company

4507 Charlotte Avenue
Suite 100
Nashville, Tennessee 37209
(615) 255-2665

www.turnerpublishing.com

Printed in the United States of America

08 09 10 11 12 13 14 15—0 9 8 7 6 5 4 3 2 1

For Gary, Venus, and Meade

Acknowledgments

I'd like to thank publisher Todd Bottorff for his wisdom, enthusiasm, and encouragement while I wrote this book. It was truly a collaborative project. Steven Cox's creative editing and Sean Kinch's careful reading of an early manuscript greatly improved the final version—thank you. I recognize with gratitude the work of Seamus Heaney, Burton Raffel, and David Wright, whose translations of Beowulf guided my own retelling. I am also grateful to my family for their patience, and for welcoming me back into the tribe after I finished writing about this one. Finally, thanks to Susan Eaddy, Brenna Hansen, and Cheryl Jackson for their support throughout the process; and to the lovely and inspiring Gemma Bridges-Lyman and April Scott, my very own "ladies of the loom."

A Note on Spelling

The original Beowulf began as an oral tale sometime between 700 and 1,000 a.d., and was written down for the first time about 1,000 years ago. Because the story was initially written in Old English, the spelling of "Wealtheow"—like that of all the characters' names—has varied according to translation. The spelling in this book was chosen for its clarity to modern readers.

Chapter One

There is a saying among our people: The world changes as we do, yet it is ever the same. When I was a child, this paradox was beyond my understanding. Now that I am grown, a woman looking back at her life, I see how the tales we tell create our world. What we believe about ourselves transforms us, and our actions weave a story whose significance alters with time. To be sure, the notions that guide a princess of fifteen are not what matter to the mother of a people.

It was the event of a lifetime, a royal wedding more magnificent than any ever seen. The guests murmured as the royal storyteller took his place in the center of the room.

"Hear my tale, O gods, and bless the telling," he exclaimed, lifting his arms into the air. I peered at him through a gap between the curtained door and the wall, observing from the safety of the antechamber. Though the multitude of warriors and their ladies listened politely to the poet's tale, I knew it was me they had gathered to see. At this most important moment of my life, the world would be watching.

I leaned forward against the curtain, opening it a bit wider. Lady Muni, my closest friend, looked over my shoulder in awe.

"The greatest meadhall in the world," she whispered, impressed. "And all for you. There must be hundreds of people. The poets will be singing of this for years to come."

"I can't do it," I said feebly.

Muni put her arm around my shoulders. "You have been preparing for this day since you could talk," she reassured me.

"Wealtheow," Mother called. I turned quickly and the curtain fell back into place.

"Coming, Mother," I replied. Muni and I hurried to the far side of the antechamber, where the ladies of my retinue stood waiting. Reaching up, I checked again to be sure the unfamiliar bridal crown was still there.

"I will set that straight," Mother said. I shifted restlessly as she adjusted the flowered circlet.

"The dress is gorgeous," she said, stepping back to look at me as the ladies murmured agreement. "Nearly the color of the sea."

The gown was beautiful, and I glanced down to admire its soft blue sheen. A gift from my betrothed, it was only the second item of silk I had ever worn. The first, my ceremonial cloak, the ladies placed carefully around my shoulders and fastened at my throat with a filigreed brooch.

As we made the final adjustments, I pictured again the magnificent hall and the crowd waiting for me there. I did not know this place, and I did not know these people. Everyone would say I was the most fortunate bride in the world to marry such a warrior, to join a clan as powerful as the Danes. It was the greatest honor imaginable.

Yet I had been content as princess of the Helmings. We did not live as lavishly or conquer as fiercely, but I had all that I wanted.

I smoothed a wrinkle in my skirt and sighed. Now, whether I wanted it or not, it appeared I was to have much more.

"Gorgeous," Mother repeated, smiling at me. "King Hrothgar is generous—and fortunate."

"Mostly generous," I said, looking down at the trailing hem of the dress. I twirled and the gown rose like a sail on the wind. "It will be good for dancing," I said, extending my hand to Muni. She took it with a laugh, and we spun around before the ladies could protest.

"Wealtheow," Mother said. "It is time. Remember who you are." Reaching up, she readjusted the bridal crown and said, "Be sure to speak clearly, slowly, and loudly."

"Yes, Mother," I replied, holding my chin up and straightening my back. The ladies and I followed her solemnly to the curtained door between the rooms.

"The Princess has arrived," she told the guard on the other side of the curtain. Blood sounded in my ears as the warrior moved away to alert the king. Moments passed, and a compelling voice rose above the music. The great hall fell silent.

"Loyal Danes and faithful Helmings," the king announced. "Today is a great day. No longer will our differences divide us, or the threat of war darken our days like summer storm. With the royal binding of Hrothgar king of the Danes and Wealtheow princess of the Helmings, today, my friends and allies, our houses will be joined and we will all be brothers."

The cheering multitude grew suddenly louder as the curtain was drawn aside. I felt Mother's hand on my back as she gave me a gentle push into the room. "Courage," she whispered.

I entered as in a dream.

Muni had not exaggerated—Heorot truly was the greatest meadhall in the world. Its treasures of gold, silver, and bronze were envied by all and rivaled by none. Giant beams rose up to the darkness of the immense thatched roof, while richly painted pillars gleamed in the lamplight. A huge fire crackled in the center of the room, the glow of the flames reflecting majesty everywhere.

The warriors and ladies murmured approval as I made my way slowly to the center of the great room. Firelight shimmered in the crystal pendants set in drops of silver around my neck. Twisted gold glinted from my arms and fingers. I felt gilded, like the strange statues our warriors brought back from summertime excursions.

But for all my ornamentation, the hall itself blazed brighter still, burning with the glory of the Danes. On a raised dais against the wall, its finest treasure—my betrothed—waited expectantly before the golden throne. Beside him rested another, smaller seat embedded with jewels of red and blue. The queen's chair.

For an instant I saw Mother's face smiling at me, and the faces of our small Helming retinue. As expected, all others were strangers—including my husband-to-be.

I first laid eyes on Hrothgar when the spring was in full flower. He had come to negotiate the bride price with my father. I was fifteen, of a marriageable age, and my hand appeared the natural balm for healing the conflict between our nations. Hrothgar was forty, a veteran of war—but not, it seemed, of love: His first queen had died more than ten years ago. He had no children, no direct heirs to the throne. That, Mother said, would be for me to provide.

I had always known it would be my wyrd to leave Helming. Muni was right—I had been preparing for this all my life. But it had seemed little more than playacting until the day I attended Hrothgar in my father's house. My cheeks burned with his gaze as I offered round the silver cup and spoke well-rehearsed words of peace.

He watched me as the diplomats regaled him with my virtues, assuring him of my ability to bear children. I kept my eyes fixed on the cup, recalling how often I had heard his name spoken in fear. It required no one to convince me that the king of the Danes was the most powerful warrior in our world.

The summer passed in frantic preparation, and then I bid my father and brothers farewell, said good-bye to the forests I loved, and set out on the journey to Heorot. For a week we traveled through deep forests whose leaves hinted at autumn. Traversing lonely plains and the ocean's shimmering shore, I found myself alternately elated at the adventure ahead and fearful of the unknown.

When we arrived at last, the king of the Danes himself welcomed the retinue with generous gifts and warm words of greeting. The Danish people had been hospitable and kind, eager to provide us with every necessity. We were shown to the women's quarters—"Built for you," Mother reminded me—and I spent my last night as a Helming princess, restless in a luxurious but unfamiliar bed.

Preparations for the wedding began before sunrise. I bathed under the ladies' meticulous supervision, and a maid washed my pale, waist-length hair. Scented oils were applied to my skin as Mother and the older ladies sang the rituals of fertility to the goddess Freyja. They spoke to me at length about a wife's duties to her husband. I knew about coupling, but I had imagined it to be the same for people as it was for animals, and I was surprised to learn that skills were required. I listened carefully to the ladies' descriptions of what to do and tried to picture the actions they described, alternately amused and anxious about my ability to carry out their instructions.

Now those images came unbidden into my mind as the king held out his hand and I stepped carefully onto the platform. My stomach tightened. The smoke from the fire made its way up hazily to the ceiling, and the cheering crowd seemed to sway. I felt unsteady, as though standing on the edge of one of this land's famous cliffs—my old life gone and a perilous new one before me.

I took a breath and shook my head. I must not falter. But was it truly my wyrd to wed this fearsome warrior? Even among our people, for whom death in combat was an unquestioned part of life, Hrothgar's reputation for bloodshed was legendary. Would I be able to live amid so much killing?

Gripped by these thoughts, I was unaware of the king's gaze until he leaned his head down next to mine and said, "Here now, Princess."

Startled, I stared at his clean-shaven face, the resolute jaw and calm eyes. His mouth curved into the beginnings of a smile. Marriage would not unsettle this warrior. "You are not about to be executed, my lady," he whispered. I exhaled slowly and took another breath, reminding myself that I, too, had been raised to face fear.

Hrothgar raised his arm into the air and the applause faded into expectant silence. My heartbeat left my head as he turned to me and pronounced, "I, Hrothgar king of the Danes, pledge myself to you, Wealtheow of the Helmings, and take you to be my wife. I will provide for you, and protect you and our children. Let the gods hear and the people recount this day when our own time has long passed. May Odin, father of all gods, bless this union."

And then it was my turn to repeat the ritual. I was glad to hear the words come slowly and clearly, just as Mother had counseled.

Esher, the king's most trusted advisor, stepped forward and handed Hrothgar an ancient, gilded sword. Turning to me, the king said, "Take and treasure this heirloom, sword of my father, the great Healfdene."

I made the formal bow, accepted the weapon carefully, and handed it to Mother. She solemnly exchanged it for a sharp, gleaming blade that I presented to Hrothgar. "May this sword of my father's father, the noble Wylf, serve you well," I said. He accepted it gracefully.

I felt relief as the ceremony came to its close. Reciting the ceremonial blessing of the mead, Hrothgar and I exchanged toasts— he to Odin, I to Freyja—and sipped the warm, fragrant mead from the loving cup.

At last, Hrothgar removed my bridal crown and replaced it with the queen's golden circlet. He took my hands in his and we spoke the words together. "May Var, goddess of the promise, hear our oath and bless this joining." The king smiled and I dropped my eyes, but returned the smile.

We were husband and wife.

"Let the wedding feast begin," Hrothgar proclaimed, and Danes and Helmings alike cheered as tables were brought forth and servants lay down a feast of beef, boar, and fish, along with dark bread and nettle soup.

Hrothgar and I sat together on the throneseats while the storyteller played his harp and sang of the royal lineage: the great Shield Sheafing, who rose from foundling to founder of a nation; his son, the worthy Beow, whose fame spread through the world like flame; mighty Healfdene, war veteran and conqueror of men; and finally the good king Hrothgar, wise warrior loved by many and feared by most, builder of the greatest hall the world had ever seen.

As the storyteller told his tale, I studied the man beside me, covertly admiring the lustrous red hair tied back with the traditional band. I wondered how those locks would look loose upon his shoulders. For nearly an entire verse I stared at the side of the king's rugged face, and for another, at the strong hand wrapped around the mead cup.

When the song ended, Hrothgar turned to me casually, as though the poet had been singing of some other warrior of legend—not himself—and said, "I have heard that storytelling is dear to the Helmings. Your poet is quite renowned."

"Yes, my lord," I replied, emboldened, I suppose, by the mead. "But no storyteller can equal the poet of Heorot, just as no hall is its equal—and no king."

Hrothgar smiled and refilled my cup. After a few moments, he said, "Heorot deserves its reputation—though my new queen outshines it by far."

He leaned forward and gazed at me intently. "Beautiful and gifted, they say. Worthy of making peace."

I blushed, pleased but unsettled by his frankness.

"I thank you for those words, my lord," I replied. "I pray that I may live up to them."

The royal advisor approached and Hrothgar said, "Esher, am I not the envy of every warrior in this hall? The goddess of love has smiled on me today!"

Esher smiled. "Even Freyja might be feeling a bit envious today, my lord," he replied with a friendly glance in my direction.

Hrothgar said, "You do not know it, my lady, but you are the fulfillment of a prophecy. Esher's wife is our seer and our healer, and what the Lady Eir sees always comes to pass."

"What did she see?" I asked, curious.

"A noblewoman who will bring great change to our nation," Esher answered.

"The mother of a formidable son," Hrothgar added keenly.

I was saved from having to respond to this intimation by the musicians, who struck up the first notes of the dance. Without thought, I rose out of my seat.

Hrothgar looked amused. "You'll excuse us, Esher," he said, standing and taking my hand. "It appears we are off to the dance."

Musicians played bone flute and lyre while spectators clapped and stomped their feet. Hrothgar spun me round and round as I had spun the Lady Muni only a few hours before. It seemed a lifetime ago. As we danced, my ornaments jingled madly and Hrothgar grinned. I laughed till I could hardly breathe.

Resting between dances, we listened to the poet's stories and I greeted the many Danish chieftains and their ladies who had traveled to Heorot for the wedding. We drank toast after toast to the future of the Danes. I found this sudden shift in loyalties disorienting; it was strange to think that these were my people now. As the cup passed round, I found myself making a quick, silent prayer for Helming.

The dancing and feasting had me feeling Freyja's magic by the time Mother appeared at my side and said, "Your wedding night is here." I rose and followed her from the great hall into the cool autumn air. Hrothgar and his attendants waited outside, ready to escort me to the king's quarters. At the door of the building, Hrothgar held my elbow carefully as I stepped across the threshold. To trip would be bad luck—and every portent counted at this critical time in our union.

Inside, I could see the firelight dancing across the carved contours of the king's bed. Gold medallions shaped in the likeness of Freyja decorated its rich dark wood. As Mother and the others began singing the song of fertility, I entered the warmth of the chamber, and my husband closed the door behind us.

We stood silently for a moment before the fire. "Yours is a handsome room," I said nervously, looking at the bed.

With an indulgent smile, Hrothgar reached out and touched my face gently, running his thumb over the curve of my cheek. I fell silent, unnerved by the caress. Sudden goose bumps rose beneath the layers of my clothing as he pulled me to him. Remembering what Mother and the ladies had told me, I leaned against his firm warrior's body and raised my lips to meet his.

Warm and wet, Hrothgar's mouth lingered on mine, then made its eager way to my ear. "Wealtheow," he breathed my name like a secret. My skin tingled where lips had forged their path. Impetuously, I reached to unfasten the tie that held his long hair. The thick, reddish locks fell around us like a curtain as he moved his mouth to mine again.

After a long moment, Hrothgar stepped back and removed his cloak, draping it across the frame of the bed. A sudden, foreign heat flushed through me as I hastened to do the same. Yet I was ever mindful of custom as he reached for the clasp at my shoulder. "The servant should do it," I said breathlessly, supposing that even on my wedding night an attendant would undress me.

"I sent her away," he replied, eyes and fingers intent on their task. I stood still as my dress fell to the floor, followed rapidly by my soft linen underdress. "There are some things a king should do himself," Hrothgar said, gazing on me with anticipation.

Dizzied and emboldened by my sudden nakedness, the cool air, his warm hands, I reached for the belt of his trousers. "And others he should have done for him," I said readily, drawing him down into the softness of the ornate bed.

10

Chapter Two

The next morning, when Hrothgar had risen and headed to the great hall, Mother and the ladies helped me prepare for the final marriage formalities. They dressed me once again in my beautiful blue silk dress and adorned me with slightly less finery than the day before. The one addition was the queen's golden circlet, which Mother placed on my head.

"How did you sleep, Daughter?" Mother asked. "Did you dream?"

I thought carefully, trying to recall exactly what images had come to me in the night. The dreams of a bride on her wedding night foretold a family's future.

"I was walking in the forest," I said. "It was nice—they were the woods of home, of Helming. It was a beautiful day, sunny and warm. Birds were singing and I looked up to see them. I saw their nest, with three birds around it—and one unhatched egg inside. Then from far away a wolf howled, and I started to flap my wings and run around as though I were a bird, too."

"The forest—a good sign," Mother said. The ladies nodded and murmured agreement as they finished placing the rings on my arms and fingers.

"And the birds—those are children," Mother smiled at me. "Three little ones—at least—for my Wealtheow. But the wolf signifies danger." She fell silent for a moment. "Remember this, Daughter. A mother—and a queen—must face peril with courage and determination."

"Yes, Mother," I said dutifully. I knew there was no avoiding fate; my new existence was proof of that. But life as princess of the Helmings had prepared me for household management and chil-drearing—not for wolves. With a 15-year-old's optimism, I hoped to avoid real danger. I had more immediate matters to ponder.

I looked down at Muni, who had stooped to fasten my shoes. She peered up at me curiously. I knew she was anxious to hear about my wedding night. The thought made me smile, and I stifled a laugh.

"We cannot escape our wyrd, Wealtheow," Mother said, giv-ing me a stern glance, "but we must always be vigilant and turn fortune toward us when we can."

"Yes, Mother," I repeated, wondering distractedly if she were thinking of her own life's path. She had been in these shoes, after all—a princess exchanged for peace.

"Ah, well," Mother sighed as Muni finished tying the leather straps around my ankles. "It is time for you to receive the king's gift. Let us go."

We proceeded to the great hall, where the last rituals of the marriage ceremony were to take place. Inside, Hrothgar waited on the dais with his advisors. Esher and the other war chieftains sat assembled on benches at the king's feet. Hrothgar's nephew, the boy Hrothulf, was also there to witness the ceremony.

"Good morning, wife." Hrothgar greeted me formally, but with warmth in his voice. I saw the warrior Unferth glance at him quickly. I recalled that Father had spoken of him before, describing the counselor as wise and loyal, but proud. He deeply valued his closeness and influence with the ruler of the Danes. Though his allegiance could not be questioned, he seemed to dislike the idea of anyone else—perhaps even the queen—getting close to Hrothgar. I wondered if he intended to make my life here difficult.

"Good morning, my lord," I replied.

"Do you find the marriage contract to your satisfaction, King Hrothgar?" Mother asked, initiating the formal ceremony.

Hrothgar rose and answered, "Yes, good queen and mother of the Helmings. I thank you." To me, he said, "To complete our bargain, I present you with these keys to my household, and with them, responsibility for the care of the people of Heorot."

"I thank you, my lord," I said. As he handed me the key ring, the king's hand touched mine, and I could not help thinking of the night before. I hesitated, then grasped the keys firmly and spoke the ritual words. "I pray that Frigga, goddess of the home, will guide me to conduct the business of your household with wisdom."

Hrothgar nodded, then turned to Esher, who handed him a gold armring set with red, blue, and amber jewels. It was beautiful! The gold appeared to have been spun into thread and then shaped into a spiral, with the glittering stones floating between the threads. Hrothgar noted my wonder as he slid the ring onto my arm with warm fingers.

"It is lovely, but you are lovelier," he said quietly so that only I could hear. Aloud he said, "Take this morning gift, and with it let our marriage contract be sealed."

"I thank you, my lord—my husband," I said, and bowed again. He smiled and inclined his head. I was now mistress of the household—and dismissed to undertake my duties.

In the antechamber, I showed Muni the beautiful gift I had just received. She admired it for a moment, then whispered, "So how was it, last night?"

I glanced over at Mother and saw that she was immersed in a discussion with one of the kitchen cooks. "I like him," I replied stealthily, keeping one eye on Mother as I spoke. "He is older, but these Danes certainly seem every bit as—" I paused, looking for the right word. "Fortitudinous," I said finally. "Every bit as fortitudinous as our Helming men." I grinned and Muni laughed out loud. Mother turned toward us and we walked hastily toward the door.

At Mother's insistence, we walked first to the kitchen, where I met the head cook and took a tour of the stock rooms. Then it was off to the weaving sheds, where the women of the village engaged in the intensive labor of transforming fleece from the community flocks into the clothing and textiles used by the king and his retinue.

I loved the smell of fleece in the spinning room, where the thread was spun then bundled in preparation for dyeing. The fibers of the flax plant were likewise worked with the drop spindles into thread for weaving linen, a far softer fabric than wool and one that was much preferred for undershirts and underdresses. The bunches of flax somehow brought to mind the image of Hrothgar removing my clothing, and I chuckled with embarrassment. Mother glanced at me sternly. Setting my face again into an expression of well-mannered interest, I nodded graciously as the women spinning the yarn stopped and bowed while we passed through the room.

Next came the dyeing area, where they stored the various plants used to color thread prior to weaving—woad for blue and weld for bright yellow, along with many different kinds of berry, bark, and lichen for creating the numerous browns and yellows, and the less common orange and red. No village in all the world had such a wealth of color. Several of the batches of thread spread out on the drying racks were of shades I had never seen.

The women stirring the vats of dye stopped to bow as we entered. "Your Highness," they said with deference. I smiled and returned the greeting, asking a few questions about their materials and mentioning some of the differences between these plants and those used by the Helmings.

At last we came to the weaving room. The largest of all the sheds, it housed a number of large looms where women stood and sang their weaving songs as they worked. I paused just inside the door and listened while they wove a spell for safety and strength into the cloth. It reminded me so much of home, the many hours I'd spent as a young girl sitting on the floor at the ladies' feet, pretending to weave on a toy loom. It was in the weaving room that I had learned the spells for happiness and courage, the songs of tradition, and the stories of the great goddesses and gods.

I continued to watch, unnoticed, as the song ended and conversation began. In the sheds of Helming, the women had talked of their lives, worked out difficulties with the help of their friends, and expressed hopes and fears for our men as they headed to the summertime battles. As the kitchen had always been for my mother, so was the weaving shed the heart of community for me. Though I was a stranger here in Heorot, the familiarity of the scene made me hopeful that I would one day feel comfortable in my new home.

In the corner of the busy room, a gentle-looking woman sat weaving the intricate tablet braid that was used to edge finer clothing. She rose quickly when we entered and gave us the formal bow.

"Good morning, my queen," she said to me, and to Mother, "Good morning, queen and mother of the Helmings. I am Eir, wife of Esher."

The other women had stopped their work to bow and make the formal greetings. "Please continue," I told them. To Eir I said, "I enjoyed the song."

"'From sheep to shirt,' as they say," she replied.

"There is magic in the weaving," I finished the old saying.

Her brown eyes regarded me kindly. There seemed an aura about her, as though familiarity with the earth's magic—the plants and spells she used for healing—had likewise imbued her with its power.

"We welcome you, Peaceweaver," Eir said.

I nodded, unsure how to respond. In giving me to Hrothgar in marriage, my father had prevented what would surely have been a devastating war for our people. Helming lacked the resources and warriors boasted by the Danes. And though they would have eventually prevailed, such prolonged fighting would have debilitated the Danish community as well.

I knew war was necessary to protect the life we built, but I could never rid myself of the disquiet it left in me. Our warriors thrived on the perpetual conflict and spoils promised by battle—it defined them. But the toil of women in kitchen, field, and shed was what truly made combat possible.

A thought came to me. Marrying Hrothgar was different from our customary women's work—it was intended to prevent war, not enable it. Despite my sadness at leaving home, I also appreciated this unusual privilege. It was a rare honor to be deemed a "peaceweaver."

"That is a lovely tablet braid," Mother said, noting my silence. She would no doubt admonish me later for "woolgathering" and coach me on how I should have responded. One of a queen's most vital skills, she always said, was her ability to communicate with wisdom and diplomacy.

"Do you also weave tapestries?" I said quickly, recovering my composure.

"Oh, yes," Eir replied, brightening. "I have heard that you are a talented tapestry maker, my queen. I would be honored to show you my work. It is one of Hrothgar and Esher's great battles as young men."

"I would love to see it," I said eagerly.

"I will check on the repast," Mother said. "Lady Muni will be in after the midday rest to help you prepare for the afternoon celebrations."

"Yes, Mother," I said dutifully, and set off with Eir to her quarters. Inside, I admired the long, narrow tapestry that lay half completed on the loom.

"The colors are beautiful," I told her.

"Thank you," Eir replied. "The forests are full of excellent plants for dyeing."

"Do you spend much time there?" I asked wistfully.

"In the woods?" Eir nodded. "I go there often to gather herbs for healing. I would be honored to have you accompany me sometime."

"I would like that," I said. "I spent much of my time in the forest, too, in Helming." Gazing at her tapestry, a question suddenly came to me. "Why are there no tapestries in the great hall? I have seen beautiful paintings and gilded treasures, but no tapestries."

"Our king will not permit it," Eir said simply.

"But I don't understand." I was confused. Tapestries were an essential part of a people's security. Their spells protected the hall. Every village had them.

"It is not for me to conjecture," Eir replied. "There have been no tapestries in the hall for more than ten years."

"It has never been mentioned?" I asked. She shook her head.

I frowned, perplexed. "Perhaps I will ask the king myself."

Eir smiled at me with a warmth I would soon grow to love. "He will explain it to his queen, I warrant."

Back in the queen's quarters for the midday rest, I lay down on the bed and gazed at the new loom in the corner, along with the baskets of brightly colored yarn next to it. The beginning of the weaving process was always filled with such optimism and energy. Imagining the end result and the response it would evoke, moving from possibility to possibility—what should I make? Tapestries were essential to the people's protection and prosperity. With the proper spells woven into the proper design, we could bring continued good fortune.

I yawned and closed my eyes. Just as the balls of yarn sat ready to be used, my new life as queen of the Danes also waited to be woven into shape. The thread of the past being spun into the present . . . the weaving of our lives determined already by unalterable wyrd, and yet reliant on us for its creation.

Muni woke me with a song, and I groaned in reluctance. "I was having such a good dream," I said. "There was a rainbow, and it was made of wool. The great goddess Freyja was weaving it into a tapestry, and she was saying, 'Wealtheow, look. Have you ever seen such weaving? Look at the pattern. Have you ever seen such glorious colors?'"

"You should definitely tell the queen your mother," Muni said. "Now come, we must get you dressed for the feast. Will you be wearing the blue silk?"

"No," I said, stretching and rising from the bed. "Red will match my armring much better." Muni pulled the dress from the clothes chest. Before my wedding, it had been my finest, the one I wore for formal occasions. Its pale red linen decorated with red, blue, and yellow braiding coordinated perfectly with the jewels of the armring.

"You look beautiful," Muni said wistfully, placing the queen's circlet on my head. "You are so lucky, Wealtheow, to be married to the king of the Danes. Even his enemies admire him."

"Enemies?" I said grandly. "I will protect him from his enemies." Muni laughed. "Let us go," I said. "There is dancing to be done." Arm in arm, we headed toward the glittering roof of the great hall.

As the second day of wedding festivities got underway, Hrothgar and I sat in our throneseats and presided over wrestling. The celebration of our joining would last another five days, with feasting, storytelling, dancing, games, and competitions. After this week-long commemoration, we would continue to drink the ceremonial mead every night for one moon, with toasts and prayers to the goddesses and gods of fertility. The honey in the mead symbolized fruitfulness and healing, and the month-long ritual—our honeymoon—served to ensure that our union would produce an heir to the throne of the Danes.

When the wrestling contest was over, Hrothgar and I awarded prizes to the champions. He glanced at me as we returned to the throneseats, and I smiled shyly.

"How did you find your household today?" he asked. "To the queen's satisfaction, I trust?"

"Yes, my lord, quite," I replied, my hand going up to the delicately woven armring I had received that morning. His eyes fell on it and he smiled.

"I thought it would suit you," he said with satisfaction. I felt a blush coming on but bravely fought it back.

"Thank you, my lord," I replied steadily. He looked at me expectantly, and I realized that he was waiting for me to speak. But what was I to say to the imposing king of the Danes—my new husband?

"Why have you not allowed tapestries in the great hall?" I asked. Hrothgar grimaced and leaned back in his seat. I chastised myself as we sat in silence for a moment, looking out over the multitude of Danes enjoying their feast and the storyteller's song. The light of the great fire shone on the ladies' jewelry and the warriors' armor, and gleamed in the gold and silver of the household treasures.

"I had a dream," he said finally, with difficulty.

"A dream about tapestries in the great hall?" I asked carefully.

"Yes," he replied, continuing to gaze out at the celebration taking place around us. "When my wife . . . the former queen . . . died in childbirth, I had a dream. Odin, the Allfather, came to me, and said, 'The magic is in the weaving. But the luck is in your queen.'"

"I am so sorry," I said softly, moved by his revelation. I had heard the queen of the Danes died young, but I had not known she was with child.

Hrothgar turned to look at me, an old pain in his eyes. "So I ordered such tapestries as there were in Heorot removed, and I vowed to wait—" Here he stopped and shook his head as if to clear his thoughts, then said slowly, "I vowed to wait for good fortune to return."

I gazed at him for a moment, pondering. It was obvious the king mourned a woman who had been dead for more than ten years. And he had lost a child.

But I was queen now. I could not concern myself with an ancient ghost. I lifted my chin determinedly. We cannot escape our wyrd, as Mother always said. The voices of the past may guide us, or they may hinder. Either way, we must do with our present what we can.

Still, it was a risk; I might have misjudged the king's temperament. But more likely, my instincts were correct, and the great warrior Hrothgar was, in fact, a man like other men—in need of comfort in times of trial. I took a breath, then reached over and put my hand on his.

"I will make a tapestry for this hall," I said, "that will bring your fortune back to you."

I had spoken well. Hrothgar looked down at my hand on his, then into my face. He turned his palm up to meet mine and said, "I know you will."

On the last day of the honeymoon, I woke with a dull dread in my heart. Today Mother would leave me to return to Helming, and I would never see her again. Muni, at least, was staying with me. She patted my arm as I lay on my bed and cried. "Here now, Wealtheow, you don't want your mother to see you like this, do you?"

I sniffed petulantly, but sat up and wiped my eyes. Muni was right. Raising her children to be rulers of nations was the most important thing in Mother's life. She had worked hard to prepare me to be a queen. I could at least repay her by acting like one.

"I'm fine now, thank you," I said with a final sniff. "I think I will wear the brown wool today."

A short time later, we emerged from the women's quarters

and walked to the stables where Mother's retinue had gathered. "Good-bye, ladies," I said warmly. "Good-bye, noble Helming warriors. You have served well, and I thank you." I turned to Mother with a trembling lip.

"Here now, my Wealtheow," she said. "You have done well for yourself. Honor the goddesses and the gods, and I will be with you when you need me."

I nodded, then replied as steadily as I could, "Safe travels, Mother. We may never see each other again in this world, but I know we will sing songs of strength and happiness together again someday."

Mother smiled and embraced me. The servants helped her onto her horse, and she raised her arm in salute. Then they were gone.

Muni and I watched until we could no longer see even the dust from the horses' hooves. I stared into the empty sky, feeling suddenly adrift. The world seemed perilous, bereft of protection.

"My queen," someone said, startling me. I wiped my eyes hastily on my sleeve and turned around. Eir smiled and made the formal bow.

"I'm sorry," she said. "I didn't mean to surprise you. I came to ask whether you would care to join me in the forest today."

A walk in the woods was exactly what I needed. The tree spirits would help ease my sadness. "Yes, thank you," I said with a sniff that she pretended not to notice.

We set off toward the south, to an area that was unfamiliar to me. I had been out with Eir a few times already, but always to the eastern woods that lay between the village and the dunes of the sea.

It was cool in the autumn shade of the forest. The yellow and orange leaves of the beeches would soon be dropping. I put my hand on the trunks of the trees as we passed by, gathering strength from their ancient spirits, and giving of my own. I prayed a blessing to each one that I touched: Be well. Grow strong. Live long.

"There is a lake here," Eir said. "It is an old place. Our elders say it is the home of great magic, of growing and healing. Would you like to see?"

"Yes," I said. She smiled at my eagerness and led the way down off the path and through a rock-strewn draw.

We came out of the forest onto a ledge of rock that hung right at the water's edge. Sunlight sparkled on the surface of the lake, reflecting the sky and the ancient trees that grew beside its calm blue-gray water. I looked down through the clear stillness to the thick green plants at the bottom. A school of silver fish darted in and out of the swaying fronds.

I took off my shoes. "Wait!" Eir said. "It's deeper than it looks."

I paused, distracted. I hadn't quite realized I intended to enter the water. On such a cool day, a swim would have been unpleasant. But the lake's pull was strong. I could feel its presence almost as tangibly as I felt Mother's absence. It seemed to emanate security and well-being.

"I am drawn to it," I told her.

"That is natural," Eir said. "There is great power here. It is a place of fertility and healing."

I looked at the giant tree next to me. Its roots curved down and around into the water. "It is our own Yggdrassil," I said, thinking of the world's creation and of the great tree from which all life sprang.

"It grows, and gives life," Eir said. "Perhaps the life is growing in you, too."

I looked at her, involuntarily putting a hand to my belly. Was she right? Could it be that I was with child? The heir to the throne of the Danes might already be among us, I found myself thinking hopefully.

Yet only the goddesses and gods know what power lies hidden in nature.

Chapter Three

"Hear my tale, O gods, and bless the telling," the cracked voice whispered to itself. But thought was simpler, and there was no one to hear the words anyway. *For the outcast would have it told, how the world ended and began again. How joy and life became pain and suffering. How we were thrust from our home and brought here by our wyrd, to the wilderness.*

It was the thirteenth year of wandering for Ginnar and her son. Sometimes it seemed a lifetime—and for him, it was. But other times she felt that she could close her eyes and be back home, her husband in the hall with his king and she in their home with her weaving.

They would kill us if they could.

In that other life, she grew up amidst the wealth and privilege of the court, and had no reason to think it would ever be otherwise. When she reached a marriageable age, she joined with one of their king's most trusted advisors. Blessed with a talent for tapestry making, she eventually became overseer of the weaving sheds for their queen. The couple knew no want, passing the days in luxury and enjoyment. What happiness when at last they found they were with child! It was good to be born into their world.

Freda, the queen—her friend—helped Ginnar plan for the arrival. Freda had her own babe now and knew what to do. The months passed in cheerful preparation—weaving and sewing the tiny clothes and soft bedding, building a cradle, pondering name after name for the son they were sure they would have. Some days, they were determined to name him for her husband's father. Other days, it seemed wisest to honor one of the uncles. So many noble warrior namesakes.

My babe was denied the naming ceremony.

With the skill that was her specialty, Ginnar wove a blanket of red and blue to swaddle the babe when it was born. There was magic in the weaving. She put all her love and joyful anticipation into the work, so that her child might know from the very first that she would always cherish him.

The seasons passed, and at last the time came. Freda stayed with her as the pains grew and the babe was born. Its cry was strong and healthy, but the queen remained strangely silent as she lay it on the floor, their people's custom. Ginnar heard her husband draw his breath.

"What is it?" she cried. Finally Freda spoke, her voice full of dread and sorrow.

"Monster," the queen said.

No. It couldn't be true. "Pick it up," Ginnar called to her husband. It was custom—if a father held a babe in his arms, it was accepted. If he did not—as was required for the sickly or malformed—it would be taken to the woods and abandoned. This could not happen to her child.

"Pick it up!" Ginnar called with rising panic. "It is crying," she said. "Pick it up!"

"It is a monster," her husband replied slowly, with poorly hidden disgust. "I cannot." He left the room. She heard him speaking with Freda outside. This could not be happening. It was a dream, a nightmare.

She had to see for herself. Quietly, so as not to interrupt the murmuring voices outside, Ginnar rose from the bed and moved stealthily to the corner where the child lay. She put a hand to her mouth as tears began to fall. Her babe. Her son. A monster.

Then, tears blinding her to reason, she picked him up. Contrary to all custom, all decency, the rules of their community, she picked him up and put his deformed body to her breast.

His little mouth searched, then latched on. Now it was done. She had rejected the laws of their people for an older, more ancient custom. As her husband and Freda came in, they gaped to see the babe in her arms.

"I have nursed," she said defiantly. "You cannot take him now."

Her husband looked away and said nothing. "We must speak to the king," Freda said, shuddering.

Ginnar remained alone with her son for the rest of the day. When darkness fell, Freda came to her. "The guards will be here in the morning to take it," she said.

"No," Ginnar begged. "Remember all I have done for you and our king. Remember the life-giving favor you owe me."

"That is why I am here," Freda replied reluctantly. "I know my debt. But I cannot stop the warriors from carrying out the law. All I can do is warn you. It is all I can do."

"I gave your babe to you," Ginnar wailed, beseeching.

Tears rose in Freda's eyes but her voice was steady. "It is all I can do," she said.

So Ginnar ran.

27

She ran all night with the babe wrapped snug against her chest. By daybreak she was exhausted, and afraid the warriors would find them. But she was young and strong, and the babe for all his . . . difference . . . was healthy, so they continued to run, keeping to thick forests where the horses could not follow.

As they fled, her mind fixed on the babe's naming ceremony. He would never have the official celebration, but he must be named. She performed the ritual as best she could alone, holding him in her arms and making the sign of the hammer of Thor above him. The birds and hidden creatures of the forest were their only witnesses.

Now her babe had a name. But they had no home. And he had no gift, an essential part of the naming ceremony. She vowed to make him one as soon as she could.

Eventually they came to the edge of a village. The residents had left food on a large stone carved with runes—an offering to appease the evil spirits and keep them away from the town. "We are their evil spirits," Ginnar realized as she ate the half-rotted food.

Had it not been summer, they would certainly have perished. As it was, she had nearly two seasons to learn how to keep them alive before the cold came—before the natural world she had relied on now threatened to destroy them, as her people had tried to destroy her son.

Autumn neared, and Ginnar spent days pulling wool by the scant handful from the fluffy sides of a flock of sheep. Her heart beat quickly anticipating the shepherd's cry, but they were not discovered. Soon she had gathered enough for her purposes.

She built a small loom that could be carried on her back and wove her babe a plain wool sack to replace the clothes he was quickly outgrowing. As she worked, she sang songs of protection and stealth, so that eyes would look past the fabric. It was his naming gift, the best she could provide.

Along with the warmth of her body, the snug bag protected her babe from the winter's chill. They slept at night in burrows with her cloak wrapped around them, draped with the bright red and blue square of welcoming blanket she had woven when life seemed so sweet.

Outside another village far away from her home, she heard the people singing in their hall while she ate the stale, hard bread from the altar. She could not hear their words, but she knew they sang of victory and treasure. "They hoard their gold and silver like dragons," she whispered with a bitterness born of want. *They hoard their love.*

In this way they wandered from village to village, until eventually her lonely, disconsolate ramblings took them into true wilderness, where no others traveled. Ginnar was relieved to discover that her tears had run out at last, that she could no longer cry. They lived in the forest for a long time, surviving on any small animals she could catch and a scavenger's diet of nuts, roots, and berries. She became adept at hiding from the bear and wild boar, and avoided even the elk and deer, until a time when her boy would be strong enough to catch the creatures for their dinner.

As months became years, she found herself wondering, What is it for? Why struggle for a survival that is worse than death? The answer shone in her boy's eyes. It was their wyrd, and surely tomorrow's promise would be worth today's pain. She had not fought so hard to keep her son alive only to see his life come to nothing. Ginnar knew there must be a greater purpose for him.

It was said that as long as he was brave, fate protected the hero whose time had not yet come. She had to believe that wyrd would guide their way. Her child was alive—he was alive and he was hers and no one could take him from her. He was all she had now. Her husband, her best friend, her king, her people—all had betrayed her, and were gone.

They would kill us, but I will not let them.

So she wove the magic, and she even carved the runes. She no longer cared for the laws of civilization. What had they to do with her and her boy? The two of them were outside the world now, set apart forever, their very nature transformed by rejection.

There was an eternal quality to this day-to-day routine—the seasons, their wyrd, the struggle for life. It was the turning of the great wheel which made them one, the stories said. All life grew from a solitary source—from the great tree, Yggdrassil, which gave life to itself and to all things.

But none of this applied to Ginnar and her boy. They were cast out, unalterably separate. They alone could give life to themselves.

So then, who would avenge this murderous cruelty? In the custom of the people, the ending of life came at a price. Who would pay for their deaths, their removal from the world?

Ginnar often dreamed the same dream. She heard her name, and the delighted laughter of children. Voices rose in celebration, and the storyteller sang a tale of victory and treasure. Each time she woke, the dying music made her whimper.

She used to sing a sweet song to her babe:

Drømde mig en drøm she nat,
um silki ok ærlik pæl.

I dreamt a dream last night,
of silk and fine fur.

But that part of her heart from which such songs of hope once sprang had dried up. Now she sang only bold spells of protection, magic to make him strong, invincible.

They would kill him, but now they cannot.

She watched him growing, and saw that soon he would be a man. She would have her recompense.

Only the goddesses and gods knew what power lay hidden in nature, but Ginnar was certain it would one day be revealed. Each dark and friendless evening was a reminder of that night when Freda said, "It is all I can do."

Chapter Four

I stood at the doorway between the antechamber and the main room of the great hall, listening to the voices rise up and disappear into the rafters. I often found myself here before a feast, suspended between these two worlds—the bustle of servants preparing the repast on one side and the raucousness of hungry warriors on the other. "Is everything in order?" I asked Muni as she came to stand beside me at the curtained door.

"Other than a sad lack of tarragon, the banquet is ready," she replied. Muni had been complaining about the seasonings used by the Danes from nearly the moment we arrived at Heorot. In the process, she had become responsible for helping me manage the kitchen. Her assistance had been invaluable since Mother's departure. After only three moons as queen of the Danes, I had at least learned to delegate well.

"Eir has promised to take you to find tarragon, or something like it," I said reassuringly. "You will teach these Danes to love Helming food."

Muni smiled agreement and handed me the ceremonial horn

cup. I took it from her carefully as the room on the other side of the curtain fell silent and Hrothgar began to speak.

"Warriors," he said. "I welcome you. Winter is upon us, and the time of togetherness is here. Today, at this new winter feast, and each day of the season, let us enjoy one another's company, and remember that we are all brothers."

The multitude cheered and I entered the main hall slowly, carrying the large silver-banded horn in both hands. I approached the dais and stood before Hrothgar with arms outstretched, cup held high.

"My king," I said. "I offer you this mead of friendship. Drink, and be generous to your warriors. Do not hesitate to give them the precious gold and silver they deserve. The gods and goddesses look fondly upon the ruler who provides for his people."

The warriors and their ladies cheered again as Hrothgar took the horn and drank. He handed it back to me and I turned toward Esher, who sat on the bench at the king's feet. One by one I offered the horn cup to Hrothgar's most trusted advisors. All but Unferth smiled as they accepted the horn and drank. That warrior merely stared solemnly ahead and sipped slowly from the ceremonial horn.

"Let the feast begin," Hrothgar cried, raising his arm in the air. Lively music rang throughout the hall, and within moments the feasting tables were in place and piled high with the evening's meal.

I sat perched on the edge of my throneseat, tapping my foot to the beat of the drums, and humming along with the lyre's familiar tune. "My queen is fond of this song," Hrothgar observed with a smile as he sat down beside me.

"I am fond of all songs, my lord," I replied merrily. "Especially when dancing, as you well know."

"I certainly do," he said with mock alarm. "I must have a word with Esher and Unferth. They did not warn me of the dangers of having a young wife who so loves to dance. I have endured battles less strenuous."

I laughed and leaned forward to taste the peppered soup a servant placed before me. It was delicious. Muni's disdain notwithstanding, Danish cuisine suited me well. And so did the Danish king, I thought boldly. I glanced sideways at Hrothgar as I drank my soup.

I was much more assured now than I had been during that terrifying wedding feast. I felt comfortable in my role as queen of the Danes, though admittedly the most challenging thing I'd had to do so far was offer round the ceremonial cup. I enjoyed the luxury of the Danish lifestyle, and Hrothgar was a good husband. He did not often solicit my advice, but he listened when I spoke, and left management of the household entirely to me. I sought to honor him by performing my tasks with grace and efficiency.

Mother had often alluded to the hard choices a queen must face, but perhaps I would be fortunate. With Frigga's protection, it might yet be a while before any such difficulties came my way.

Hrothgar looked at me and said, "The queen of the Danes is wearing her hair in the fashion of the people. It is becoming."

I put a hand to the knot of hair at the base of my neck. "Thank you, my lord," I replied. "I find there is much to appreciate in the customs of your—of our—people." Hrothgar smiled and returned to his soup.

As the musicians ended their song, I gazed across the room expectantly. The storyteller sat where he always did, in the poet's seat of honor. I could tell by the look on his expressive face that he was preparing to sing a song. His bow struck the lyre with a flourish, and like a ripple on water the sound lapped the room, leaving a keen silence in its wake.

"Hear my tale, O gods, and bless the telling," he exclaimed.

In the days of long ago,
In the great hall of the gods and goddesses,
There was one who shunned all goodness.
Loki was his name,
And he spawned
Three monstrous children.
The giant serpent Jorgunmand
Was cast out by the gods,
And his monstrous sister, Hel,
Sent below to dwell—
It is of the third,
The fearsome Fenrir,
That I sing to you now.

A wolf in seeming,
Fenrir was suffered to live
In the realm of the gods, though
Only brave Tyr dared feed him.
But soon the creature began to grow
And grow until he was larger
Than any real wolf, and
The gods were concerned.

The fates had warned in prophecy
That Fenrir would be the gods' destruction,
So twice they tried to bind him

With sturdy chains of iron.
He thought it a game and laughed
As he escaped the mighty bindings.

So the gods called on the dwarves
To fashion a fetter of magic
That would capture the monster once and for all.
Well versed in the ways of mystery,
The dwarves created Gleipnir, the deceiver—
a silken ribbon cast not in iron,
but of substance more illusory:
the sound of a cat's footfall,
the beard of a woman,
the roots of a mountain,
the senses of a bear,
the breath of a fish,
and the spittle of a bird.

Fenrir was suspicious
When they came before him with a ribbon.
He demanded a guarantee
Before he would play their game again.
So brave Tyr placed his hand
In the monster's mouth,
And smiling to themselves,
The gods bound him.

Concerned at first, then infuriated,
Fenrir discovered that he could not
Escape the dwarves' magic.
And thus the gods and goddesses were saved,

Though the same cannot be said
For Tyr's hand.
That courageous god
Fed the wolf his sacrifice,
And made good the final deception.

Now bound up in Gleipnir,
And chained to immovable rock,
Fenrir lies helpless
Until the twilight of the gods.

"That is one of my favorites," I said to Hrothgar when the song finished. "Tyr is so brave, and makes such a sacrifice."

"The one-handed god is a god of courage," he agreed. "However, I myself prefer tales of battle to those of intrigue."

Just then I heard a plaintive voice rise above the crowd. I looked down and saw the boy Hrothulf standing before the bench of advisors. "I would see the great Hrunting, my lord Unferth," he said crankily. I could tell that he was sleepy, and rose to go over to him.

"Of course, young lord," Unferth said patiently, removing the ancestral sword from its scabbard and holding it upright before him. Hrothulf stared in awe at the gleaming blade and silver-encrusted hilt. Its spell-built spirals and ancient inlaid runes assured strength and victory to the wielder.

I approached the counselors' bench and made the formal bow. "My lords," I said.

"Look, Wealtheow," Hrothulf exclaimed. "Is this not the most beautiful sword you have ever seen? It must have slain many enemies."

And a few friends, I thought to myself, recalling the kitchen gossip. Muni said that Unferth's brothers had died by his own hand. Because he was a brave warrior and treasured advisor to the king, such rumors were not spoken aloud in the hall, but rather whispered in the kitchen and smithy.

"Its tales are many," Unferth replied with a glance toward the throne, where Hrothgar sat in conference with a chieftain. "Perhaps some day I will tell them to you, young lord."

"My uncle the king has his stories told the world over," Hrothulf bragged. "I will be a great warrior and storyteller someday, too." By his tone, it was clear the boy's imagination was about to surpass reality in this impromptu speech. "I am learning the sword," he continued, gathering speed, "and even now I sing glorious tales of my uncle's victories."

Unferth sheathed the great sword Hrunting and gazed on the boy impassively. "It requires more than poetry to make a great warrior," he said. "But by all means, young lord, recite for us a 'glorious tale' of your uncle." Hrothulf opened his mouth, then paused. He looked up at me helplessly, and I realized he had no story to recite before the advisors.

It would humiliate Hrothulf to have to admit his empty boasting—a valuable lesson I would normally condone. But for such humiliation to come at Unferth's hand—that was another matter. It did not seem wise to allow the counselor to gain even this small advantage over Hrothgar's nephew.

Thinking quickly, I said, "Here now, my lord Hrothulf. The hour is long past for your retiring. Would it not be better to honor these mighty warriors with a fresh rendering of your poem tomorrow at dinner?"

Unferth's gaze hardened as I spoke, but the worthy Esher agreed, saying, "Indeed, even the bravest warrior needs his rest. You may speak to us again tomorrow, my young lord."

Odin bless him, Hrothulf had the presence of mind to make a formal bow. I did likewise and then whispered, "Come, let us bid goodnight to your uncle the king."

As we made our way to the dais, Hrothulf said gratefully, "You are as beautiful and wise as Freyja, Wealtheow. I think I will call you Aunt Wal." I looked down at him, startled, then laughed.

"And you are as charming and mischievous as Loki the trickster, my lord Hrothulf," I replied, patting his head. "I am honored by my new name. But in the future, it would be wise not to promise more than you can produce." He nodded and stifled a yawn as we approached Hrothgar.

"I come to wish you goodnight, my lord," I said with a smile. "Hrothulf is in need of his 'Aunt Wal.'"

"'Aunt Wal'?" Hrothgar repeated, amused. "Very well. Goodnight." As I turned to go, however, he said, "A moment, my queen." I stopped, puzzled by the hesitation in his voice. The king of the Danes was rarely indecisive.

"I have long intended to ask you," he said. "How proceeds your weaving?"

I knew he referred to the tapestry in progress in my quarters. Traditionally, a king rarely visited the queen's private domain, and Hrothgar had not yet been invited. "It goes well, my lord," I replied. Then, impulsively, "You should come see it . . . that is, it would be . . . my lord is welcome to observe my work at his will," I finished weakly.

"Very well," he said, apparently satisfied. "Goodnight." I made the formal bow and took Hrothulf by the hand.

"Tomorrow you will recite your poem before the warriors," I told the sleepy boy cheerfully as we left the hall. "I know it will be wonderful. But you must practice very hard."

39

The next morning, as I regarded the tapestry's bright colors and contemplated which shades of yellow and brown I should use for the thatched roof of Heorot, a servant entered to announce the king.

I had made excellent progress on the weaving. Creating a tapestry for the great hall consumed a large portion of my time and thought. What daylight I did not spend overseeing the weaving sheds or kitchen, or searching the forest for herbs with Eir, I spent at the loom in the queen's quarters.

The delicately woven scene that was unfolding, though only partly finished, would be the most remarkable I had ever created—I was sure of it. A depiction of Hrothgar's construction of Heorot, the long narrow banner was intended as part of a series of panels that would hang one above the other to tell the story of the king's rise to power and subsequent triumphs. I had relied heavily on Eir for details of times past, but my inspiration came entirely from Hrothgar. I wanted to give him a tapestry worthy of a great hall—and a great king. I longed to bring his good fortune back to him.

But this was not all I hoped to give him. I knew it was past time to speak with Hrothgar about an important matter, though till now an unexpected timidity had held me back.

I smoothed my hair with my hands and adjusted the necklace of gems and gold pendants that hung around my neck. "Please tell the king I would be honored to have him enter," I told the servant, who bowed and left the room.

Hrothgar came in slowly, seemingly conscious of his status as a visitor to these rooms. We greeted one another and he approached the tapestry to examine its fine detail. He stepped back to admire the whole, and smiled as he recognized the story unfolding there.

"It is beautiful," he said.

"Thank you, my lord," I replied. "As you can see, there is still much to be done."

"That is ever the way," he said, then leaned forward to peer at a tiny figure and horse. "I was not aware I had quite that much hair," he said seriously.

"Oh yes, my lord," I replied. "Your lustrous locks are the talk of Heorot." He chuckled.

"My lord, I—" I said and stopped. I sat down on the bench beside the weaving loom and glanced up at him. My heart began to race and I felt breathless.

"What is it?" he said. "Do not be wary. You can speak to me of whatever you wish."

"Hrothgar," I said slowly, "I am with child."

For several weeks, I had been feeling weary and nauseated, but had tried to ignore it. Finally I went to Eir for something to settle my stomach.

She had examined me and asked a few questions, then reflected thoughtfully on my answers. "Why did you not come to me about this earlier?" she asked.

I had not thought myself in need of a remedy because I assumed the sickness was a temporary result of my . . . intimacy . . . with Hrothgar.

"It is," she laughed gently when I explained. "But not just because you have been together—you are going to have a baby."

At my words, Hrothgar's eyes widened and he dropped down on one knee beside me. "So soon," he breathed. "This is wonderful." He put his arm around me, and I leaned against him, breathing in the familiar smell of leather and scented oils.

"We will make the announcement at Yule," he said suddenly, jumping up. I laughed to see him so excited. This was the first time I had witnessed such emotion from the king of the Danes.

"Here now, do you laugh at the father of your child?" he demanded.

"Oh no, my lord," I said. "I was only remembering a tale the storyteller told last night, the amusing one about Freyja and the necklace of the Brisings."

He knelt down beside me again. "Wealtheow," he said. "What can I do for you? Have you any need?"

I smiled and patted his knee much as I had patted the boy Hrothulf's head the night before. "I thank you, my lord," I said. "But my home is the greatest meadhall on earth, and my husband its noblest warrior and king. My companions are treasured and faithful. And summer will bring us a child. I truly have all that I could want."

Chapter Five

The Yule celebration was the most important and exciting of the winter. Seven days of revelry marked the longest night of the year, and thus the beginning of the sun's return. First, we lighted the giant Yule log, which burned throughout the festival, and offered a prayer to Thor, protector of the hearth. Next came the sacrifice of the finest boar, on which the warriors swore their allegiance to the king. Once the flesh was roasted, festivities began in earnest.

A moon had passed since I told Hrothgar our good news. Only Esher, Eir, and Muni knew that an heir to the throne was expected, but after tonight the news would fly across the nation. As the feast of the boar began, Hrothgar stood to give the traditional speech.

"Friends and brothers," he said. "We gather together at this Yuletide feast to remember that we are one people—a strong people. We assemble to chase out the night and welcome back the day." The crowd cheered. Hrothgar turned to look at me, then back to the multitude.

"I have wonderful news for the Danish kingdom," he said.

"Today we celebrate not just the returning of the light, but the coming of an heir to the Danish throne." In a few seconds the words sank in and a loud cheer went up, rippling through the crowd and growing louder as it spread. Hrothgar raised his arm for silence and gradually the happy shouts subsided.

"To commemorate this joyful occasion," he announced, "every inhabitant of Heorot will receive a gift of silver or gold from the king's storerooms." Another wave of cheering ensued. Hrothgar took my hand and we stood before the people, smiling at each other and at the crowd.

"In addition to the babe itself," Hrothgar said later, when the feasting had begun, "there is another fortunate result of the coming of a child." I looked at him quizzically. "Less dancing," he said with a grin.

"Ha!" I replied. "That is what you think." I stood and held out my hand. Hrothgar sighed, then gave the formal bow and led me to the dance.

And so the week of Yule proceeded. We feasted, danced, sang, and listened to the storyteller's best yuletide tales. We enjoyed the warriors' friendly flytings—insult contests—and humorous competitions to tell the most preposterous story of heroes and magic. The mead flowed, and the people were happy.

Hrothulf was especially excited. Yule was a traditional time of gift giving—or rather, receiving—for the children of the Danes. The boy's parents had died years ago, and so it was for Hrothgar to provide him with a Yule gift.

"Perhaps a dog," Hrothgar mused.

"Perhaps a sword," I said, remembering our nephew's excitement over Hrunting. "Though he is but nine years old."

"He will grow into it," the king replied, nodding thoughtfully at my suggestion. "He is already in training with the weapons master."

We looked across the room to where Hrothulf played at wrestling with another boy. "Perhaps a sword and a dog," I said. "Eir's bitch has just had pups."

Hrothgar smiled. "Something tells me our child will be quite indulged," he said.

"A boy needs a sword and a dog," I insisted. "Both will protect him from danger."

"As long as he can keep the two apart," he replied, and I laughed.

It was the seventh and final day of the celebration. The servants had constructed an enormous bonfire outside the great hall, and the crowd now assembled in the ring of gathering. Hrothgar and I sat in specially constructed thrones on a small stage to one side of the fire. The gilded throneseats shone in the light of the giant blaze. Hrothulf sat beside us, bouncing up and down excitedly in anticipation of the annual recounting of Odin's Wild Hunt.

"Hear my tale, O gods, and bless the telling," the storyteller began.

"On this night, the Wild Hunt is at its peak. Odin the Allfather rides the wind on the great eight-legged Sleipnir, the fastest horse alive—or dead. Attended by shadowy horsemen and baying hounds, the Allfather's horn peals through the night and draws away to death all who see or hear him."

As he told the familiar story, I recalled how I had enjoyed this eerie tale as a child. It was strange—and wonderful—to think on how my own babe would someday take pleasure in it, too. I felt acutely aware of the turning of the great wheel, the familiar repetition of seasons and rituals—the comfort and security of wyrd making its way through the world.

"At this time of renewal," the storyteller concluded, "when the sun prepares to be reborn and shine again upon us, we celebrate the light. We pray to the gods and goddesses for protection and strength on this, the longest night." He made a gesture toward the bonfire, and a giant explosion of sparks flew up to the heavens.

"Hurrah!" Hrothulf exclaimed with excitement. "Hurrah!"

I smiled as he turned to me and said hurriedly, "Goodnight, Aunt Wal. I must put hay outside for Sleipnir so the Allfather will pass us by without blowing his horn." I wished him a good night and watched as the children of the Danes were sent to bed.

When the young ones had departed, the mood of the festivities changed, becoming more serious. The drums began to beat rhythmically, and the storyteller sang a song of ancient wisdom. Then the Lord Esher entered the ring of gathering, walking slowly and ceremoniously. In his hands he carried a large rock, the telling stone, a mystic relic of the Danish people's past. Etched in its numinous surface were interwoven spirals, solar discs, and inlaid runes. I had never seen it before, but I knew the stone spoke of mysteries.

Esher proceeded to the stage and set the stone on a specially constructed podium.

"Yesterday, today, and tomorrow," he pronounced. "So the people were, so they are, and so they shall be, till the twilight of the gods." He stepped back and Hrothgar stood slowly, his arms in the air and palms facing out.

"The Lady Eir will make the reading," he said. Eir stepped forward and placed her hands slowly on the telling stone. For several moments she traced its spirals and letters with her fingers. Then she gazed into the bonfire. The immense blaze danced and spat as the drums beat rhythmically into the night. For a moment I imagined that I, too, could see the Danes' future in the flames.

Finally Eir turned to the king and spoke. The firmness of her tone surprised me. Her normally mild voice carried all the way to the edges of the multitude that crowded thickly about the stage.

"At the height of darkness, we gather to see the way," she said. The drums continued to beat, and after another moment of staring into the fire, she continued, "What is cast out will be reclaimed, but not without terrible suffering. And though much will be lost, that which has gone astray can be righted, and happiness will come again. This is what I see."

When Eir had made the divination, Esher removed the stone and the people began to dance, circling about the fire in an ever-tightening spiral, then winding back out again. Soon they would move to the great hall or to their own quarters, to spend the rest of the long night in continuing revelry or much-needed sleep. All would be indoors well before midnight—no one wanted to risk hearing Odin's horn.

I stayed and stared a while longer into the fire, searching for my own future in the flickering light. Eir's fortune-telling had not yielded favorable tidings. I must ask her about it tomorrow.

I watched dragons form in the flames, followed by a host of armored horsemen. The horsemen transformed into a hundred snakes, who in turn became waves on a lake of fire. I put an absent-minded hand to my belly. The world was full of signs and portents—we needed only to learn how to see them.

And so we passed the winter in camaraderie, the days growing longer and my belly growing larger. Preparation for the babe consumed all my thought. I had taken a break from working on the tapestry to make myself a larger dress. Eir provided me with a beautiful pale-blue yarn, and I wove my new garment with care. Such dresses were intended to last for many babes.

Next I made a colorful sack for my babe, a pretty bag of red, yellow, and blue to match the armring Hrothgar had given me. Muni and Eir wove soft bedding, and Hrothgar himself built the cradle.

The season's turning came at last, as the warmth of early spring chased away the winter's frequent fogs and mists. The drier weather was a welcome change and I began to spend more time outdoors, walking in the forest and contemplating names for our babe. Hrothgar and I had settled resolutely on Hrethric for a boy, but had more trouble with the name for a girl. I longed to honor my mother, while Hrothgar favored a name from his clan. We settled at last on Freawaru. Now we lacked only a babe to fix with these honored names.

There was much to be done in the springtime to prepare for the summer's excursions. Our warriors were also farmers, and had to plow and sow the fields before they journeyed out to battle. Our babe would be born in midsummer, and Hrothgar's first expedition would be accordingly brief so that he could return in time to meet his son or daughter.

With springtime also came the feast of Ostara, a celebration of fertility and life. Special honor was paid to those with child, and Eir presented me with an amulet of curative herbs and precious stone to mark the occasion. I wore it faithfully. Hrothgar had been right about dancing, however; during the festivities I was content to merely watch.

Muni was my constant companion as I grew in need of more help with my daily responsibilities. When we were not tending to the demands of the household, we spent quiet times in my quarters, talking of home or—more often than not—of some handsome warrior Muni admired from afar. Occasionally she told me stories or sang songs of the Helmings.

One day she surprised me with a lullaby I had not heard since I was very young. As she sang, she worked a tablet weaving of red and brown. I lay on the bed watching her fingers form the braid and listening to the sweet song.

"Where did you learn that?" I asked when she finished. "It is lovely."

"Your mother taught it to me," she replied.

"Mother taught you a song that she did not teach me?" I asked, perplexed.

She smiled but answered quite seriously, "There is much your mother taught me in preparation for my service to you." She placed her weaving on the clothes chest and stood up. "As for the tune, your mother said it helps a babe to sleep. I am to teach it to you so you can sing it to little Hrethric or Freawaru."

"It helps a mother to sleep as well," I said drowsily, closing my eyes. Suddenly, I felt a sharp pain in my stomach. I put my hand to my belly and struggled to sit up.

"What is it?" Muni asked.

"It hurts," I said, falling back on the bed as the pain coursed through my body.

"I will get Eir," Muni said, and ran out.

The babe was not due for two more moons, but it came anyway.

In the end, there was little that could be done. I labored but never saw my babe. Muni told me later it had been a boy.

Weeks passed, and I would not leave the queen's quarters. I could not bear to see the people's faces. I had failed them. And I had lost my babe.

The future seemed finished, while the present rang with sounds I would never hear. My babe's cry, his sweet voice, the laughter of a child—in the quiet of my rooms, these ghosts echoed and faded into a deep, grieving silence.

Hrothgar tried to comfort me, but he didn't know how. In truth, no one could offer any consolation. To worsen matters, the warriors would be leaving soon for the expedition. After that there would be only emptiness.

The babe had not suffered, Eir assured me.

Pushing back the sadness that ever blackened my thought, I began to reflect obsessively on preventing this from happening again. It was commonly known that the loss of an unborn babe could signify an inability to bear children. I would not let this happen to me.

At last I allowed Eir to persuade me to go for a walk in the forest, but only because I needed to discuss with her the object of my fixation. I intended to enlist her knowledge of medicine and magic to help ensure I never lost a babe again.

"Is there some potion I can take?" I asked her. "Spells I can cast? I have prayed to the gods and goddesses, and I will continue to pray. But what else can I do? There must be some other, more certain way to be sure I never lose—" Here I paused, and took a deep breath. "That this never happens again."

Eir looked at me sympathetically. "There are some small things," she said slowly. "Certain herbs will help. But in truth, my lady, it is for wyrd to guide the way. You know this. Things will be as they will be."

Her words pricked at the pain inside me. I thought hard, and we walked for a moment in silence.

"The runes," I said, stopping suddenly. "Like the telling stone! We can create an altar for the spirits of the letters and call on their protection."

Eir looked slightly alarmed, but spoke softly. "Wealtheow," she said. "It is not to be done. The agony of the writing ritual . . ." she trailed off, as though remembering.

"One must suffer horribly to achieve knowledge of the runes," she said after a moment. "Do you not recall how Odin himself hung upside down in the tree of life for nine days to receive the gift? I pray that you will never suffer that much."

"But I have suffered!" I cried. "I cannot suffer anymore."

I turned and ran into the forest. I heard Eir calling after me but I ignored her. As I fled, I sobbed until I didn't have enough breath to do both. I slowed to a walk.

Coming to a deeper part of the forest, I stopped to put my hand on an ancient trunk, in need of its comforting spirit. But I felt nothing. Holding perfectly still, I strained my senses in an effort to open myself to the life around me. I pressed my palm hard against the bark, listening. After several moments, I let my hand drop.

I could no longer hear the trees.

Numbly I walked on, paying no attention to my direction or path. I became aware of a gradual tingling sensation on my skin, as one sometimes feels when Thor throws his thunderbolt. I peered ahead through the dimming light and saw a patch of sky, a break in the trees. Moving toward it, I felt a sudden renewal of purpose.

I emerged onto the same narrow ledge where Eir and I had been before. It was the lake, the ancient water in the woods where Danish ancestors gathered to ensure the people's success and fertility.

When last I had been here, I nearly walked into its clear depths, but this time I merely went down on my knees at the water's edge.

"I have suffered," I whispered. I clasped my hands to my chest, and felt the amulet Eir had given me for Ostara. I drew its cord over my head and threw the necklace into the water. I watched the ripples from the small splash fade, then put my head into my hands and cried.

I lay in supplication there for some time, staring at the trees beside me. Their twisted roots drank deep from the ancient mere. After a while, the wind picked up and began to sing through the limbs of the forest. I sat up with a shiver and wrapped my cloak about me. As I gazed on the lake's suddenly choppy surface, there came a strange shimmer on the face of the water. Unexpectedly, as in a dream, my mother's visage appeared, surrounded by floating tresses tied up with ribbons of silver and gold.

"Mother!" I cried. "Oh, Mother!"

The watery image reached out to me, and I thought I could hear my name. "Wealtheow," she called.

"Oh, Mother, help me," I cried. "My babe is dead. It's gone—gone."

At that moment Eir rushed up behind me from out of the wood. "Wealtheow," she said. Then, glancing at the lake, she gasped in amazement. "What hydromancy is this?" she exclaimed.

At once the wind died, and the image disappeared.

I woke the next day feeling strangely lighthearted. For the first time since the loss, I looked over at the tapestry in my quarters with a twinge of interest. It hung patiently on the loom.

"You have been waiting," I said gratefully. I ran my fingers over the tiny figures of king and horse, then took up the colorful strands of wool and began to weave. Soon I was immersed in the work, dark thought chased out by the repetitive motion of my hands.

"My queen," a servant said, startling me out of my reverie. "The king begs your leave. He would speak with you."

"Of course." I stood up from the loom as the servant bowed and Hrothgar entered. I moved forward and took his outstretched hand.

"My lord," I said. He squeezed my hand and then put his arm around my waist, pulling me gently to him. I gazed up at him with mild surprise.

"My warriors and I leave soon for the South," he said into my hair. Then, "You are well?" he asked. I nodded, and realized: He had been afraid I would die. That I would perish in fatal, futile childbirth, as his first queen had so many years ago.

I rubbed my cheek against the linen of his shirt. "I am well," I replied reassuringly, and in saying so, recognized that it might be true.

Hrothgar looked down at me tenderly and said, "I am glad." In his eyes I observed a new shadow, evidence of lingering grief. I was not the only one who had lost a child.

How could I let him know we felt the same pain?

"I will wash your hair," I said impulsively. The king's expression changed, and he looked almost bashful for a moment.

"My mother always did it for my father before he left for the excursions," I said. "It is good luck."

"It has been a long time," he replied. "I might not remember how to have my hair washed by a woman."

"I will help you remember," I said, reaching for a red-gold strand. "You will enjoy it, I promise."

And he did.

All of Heorot gathered in the early summer sunshine to see the warriors off. The warhorses stamped eagerly, the gold and bronze mounts of their bridles jingling and glinting in the morning sunlight.

Dressed in their battle gear and armed with sword, spear, and axe, the Danish warriors were a magnificent sight. Their crested iron helmets were set with polished bronze, and the silver-gray chains of their neck guards and mail shirts clinked impressively as they mounted the horses. Every warrior wore a long-bladed sword slung from his belt, its gleaming hilt encrusted with silver or gold.

Servants handed up the sharp spears along with round shields painted red with the snarling symbol of the Danes. To the enemy, these warriors were the most terrifying spectacle they had ever seen. To us, they were glorious—mighty protectors of the Danish kingdom.

The most splendid of them all, Hrothgar gazed down at me from astride his impatient mount. "It will be a short trip," he assured me. "We will return by the next moon."

I nodded silently and raised my arm in farewell. As we watched them ride away to the South, I forced back an unwelcome fear.

The tribes they traveled to meet were small, but fierce. Recurring raids on the outskirts of the kingdom—a week's ride from Heorot—had grown bolder over the past few summers, and had to be stopped.

It was a routine excursion, I told myself, like dozens I had witnessed in Helming. And yet this one was different—it was taking my husband away from me. I felt the tears rise and shook my head vehemently, warning them back.

He would return. He must return.

I had a dream that night. Mother appeared in flowing white robes, her hair tied up with gold and silver rope, her arms entwined in braided gold rings. She spoke to me, and her voice sounded like water. "The chest, my daughter," she said. "You will find the aid you seek."

When I woke the next morning, I lay in bed for several suspended moments, remembering my dream. As I rose finally and looked around the room, my eyes fell on the clothes chest I had brought with me from Helming. My heart jumped.

I went over to the chest and slowly opened the lid. Reaching down past the dresses and underdresses and cloaks, I felt all around and pressed my hand against the flat wooden bottom. Nothing.

I explored each corner of the chest with my fingers. On the final corner, my fingertip brushed a tiny raised edge. I put my fingernail under it and pried up a thin, narrow strip of wood. Quickly, excitedly, I threw all the clothes out of the chest and pulled up the false bottom I had never known existed.

And there, at the true bottom, lay a small bundle of vividly woven fabric. I picked it up and stretched it out to its full length in my hands. It was a girdle of remarkable loveliness, a hand's span in width and long enough to wrap around the waist, with long narrow ribbons for tying. Its intricate waves of delicate blue and red wool danced upon a mere of golden silk. I rubbed its softness between my fingers, amazed at this mysterious treasure. It was the most beautifully woven item I had ever seen, more beautiful even than my wedding dress of sea-blue silk.

Muni entered the room with the breakfast tray. She set it down on a bench and I turned to her, the girdle still stretched between my hands. She caught her breath and clasped her hands, then exhaled slowly.

"I can tell you what that is," she said.

Chapter Six

Hear my tale, O gods, and bless the telling. Ginnar the wanderer has only herself to talk to these days. My boy no longer cares for the stories.

When she was with the people, there were rites of passage for a boy's coming of age. He would ascend to manhood with a trial and a blessing and the gifts of the clan. Her boy had had a lifetime of trial. Instead of blessing, she would mark his transformation with a curse on those who cast them out. For a gift, she would give him purpose he could not find here in the wilderness.

He was growing. Her boy did what the children of the people could never do. He was faster and stronger. He was a better hunter. Be it bear, boar, or elk, there was no animal he could not fell. He would have made a fearsome warrior.

Her boy was growing. She watched him sometimes when he slept, curled around his latest kill. It brought to mind years past, when he was closer to babe than to man. How he had loved to run and play in the forest! Climbing trees, swimming streams, stalking small prey . . . to watch him hunt was to observe the graceful conquest of one animal over another.

That's what they were now, animals. Her boy brought the warm carcass to their lair and they ripped it apart with their hands, gnawing bloody, delicious limbs with no concern for manners or appearance. To eat was to survive; there was no shame in it.

It was hard at first to stomach the uncooked meat, but fires were too risky while they remained in the world of people. By the time they came to the wilderness, her taste for cooked flesh was gone.

Nor had they any need for the fire's warmth. She used her magic to toughen their hides, making them hardier, more resistant to the elements. Eventually they had no need even for clothes, and shed that last vestige of civilization as a snake sheds its skin. Their shiny newness was the callused, leathered product of a life spent under the sky.

Though she no longer needed them for protection, Ginnar nevertheless kept some of the old things. Her boy's naming gift— the bag that kept him snug when they were first cast out—she used for carrying small stones and plants for spells and healing. And the welcome blanket she made for her babe so long ago, in that other world—she could not bear to part with it, not because it reminded her of good times before her people turned on her, but because there was magic in the weaving. She kept the ragged square of fabric folded and fastened at her waist with a sinew. The dirty threads still gleamed with anticipation and joy. Happiness that was no more.

Of course these were not thoughts she could share with her boy. He knew only one way to be. Another way would never occur to him.

When he was younger, she told him many of the stories of their people. In moments of longing, she would recount a humorous or warm-hearted tale, though she soon discovered that he did not understand it. Later she told only those that showed the people for who they were. These stories of cruelty and evil were easier for him to comprehend.

As she nurtured him, so too did she nurture her resentment of those who betrayed her, and foster her boy's mistrust of the people. It was for their own protection.

Her stories must have made it plain. He never seemed to wonder why they were here. Why they were the only ones.

When he was younger, her only joy in life was watching him grow, making him strong with her magic and tales of injustice. But storytelling was a thing of the past. Lately he did not even want to look at her. He had become restless, dissatisfied. Ginnar didn't understand how she had wronged him.

And she could no longer manage him. She used spells, runes, to no avail. The magic that rose in him was like the tide, too strong to contain.

He began to roam. He disappeared for days at a time, and she was frantic. "You cannot leave me," she cried each time he returned. Her boy only shrugged and looked away.

One winter, he was gone for nearly a moon. Lonely and distraught with worry—though the wilderness knew there was no beast that could harm him—she ceased to eat or even move about. She crawled into their burrow and fell into a dreamless sleep.

When her boy returned, he thought she was dead. Only his insistent shaking and screams roused her. He whimpered then like a baby, and let her hold him as he hadn't in a long time.

It was good that it happened. The fear would keep him beside her just a little longer—long enough to achieve her purpose, and give him his.

This boy had been her reason for living, but she saw now she could not fight the moon and hold him forever. He needed more than the wilderness could provide.

After a lifetime of sacrifice and struggle to keep him, she would still lose her babe after all. But not before she received recompense for the life that was taken from them. She called on wyrd to guide their way.

And so they returned to the land of the people.

It was not easy, forcing herself into the light of civilization. Her boy, on the other hand, was curious, eager.

They spent some time getting used to the need to hide. He was naturally good at not being seen, in part from the spells she cast and in part from having spent his life as a creature of the wilderness.

Even though they saw no people, there were traces in the forest now and then, and once her boy smelled something unfamiliar on the air. Human, she told him, and he wrinkled his nose.

Over weeks, they moved closer to populated areas, traveling by night and sleeping by day. Spring was upon them when they came to the flat fertile farmlands and rich meadows of the people. The budding loveliness was nothing like the briars and tangles of the wild, but Ginnar had brought the dark heart of the wilderness with her.

She would never forget the first time her boy heard singing. It was the closest they had been to a village, though they were still too far away to be perceived. As they loped through a meadow, the wind shifted and voices came wafting across the night air.

Her boy was stopped cold, listening alertly to the sound. He stood frozen for several moments, then turned and fled to their lair, where he lay curled with his hands over his ears. Ginnar couldn't understand why the singing hurt him.

The next time they heard it, he did not run away, though it

seemed that he wanted to. He could not at first make out what they were saying—he had never heard any voice but her own. Eventually he was able to discern meaning; then after that, when they heard the proud voices in the night, he would stop and grimace as though in pain. But he would listen.

Summer was nearing its height when they found the abandoned village. Creeping stealthily to snatch the food placed on the outskirts of town, she paused. Something was wrong. It wasn't just the lack of arrogant song; it was a deadness she could, after a moment, smell.

Ginnar ran back to their hiding place to get her boy, who had not come with her to the altar. He did not care for the people's food. She called him in the woods with the howling signal they had created when he was younger. After a few moments he bounded to her, mouth still bloody from the night's kill.

It was a full moon.

They sneaked quietly toward the village, but it was soon obvious that there was no need for stealth. The massacred inhabitants lay strewn about, unhappy victims of an enemy raid. There were few bodies of women and children, for it was not the people's way to kill them in battle. She surmised they had been taken to serve their captors.

Ginnar and her boy searched quickly to be sure no life remained.

It appeared the attack had occurred many days ago, but care must be taken lest the marauders still lurked in the area.

Entering the domain of people, they came into a world of dreams. This was a smaller village than her home, but it was civilization. Her boy had never been this near a building in his life.

Ginnar paused to look down at a warrior's swollen face in the moonlight. She had not seen another person close-up in fourteen years, and her boy had never before laid eyes on anyone but his

mother. She had forgotten how smooth humans were, how delicate. She knew, though rarely pondered, that her own visage had
changed.

When they were certain there were no living humans, she insisted that he drag the bodies to the edge of town before they
explored further. She didn't mind the stench, but their handsome
faces made her uneasy. And she didn't want to touch them, but
her boy had no such compunction.

There should be a funeral ritual, a pyre—at the very least, a
prayer to the gods and goddesses, she thought. Gods of the dirt.
A prayer to the worms. She turned quickly and left her boy squat-
ting over a corpse. How fitting that this pile of broken bodies
should be his first taste of civilization.

After a moment, he came to her and they entered the hall,
cautious though they knew no one breathed there. Their keen
night vision and the moonbeams shining through the violated
doorways were all they needed to see inside. They moved slowly
into the room.

Despite the damage of battle, the hall was magnificent. Her
boy gaped at the roof above his head, the painted timbers rising
up like magic trees. Plainly the marauders had taken the hall's
treasures, but the building itself remained. It was wrecked, but
astonishing to their wild eyes.

The feasting tables were set with stale food. Ginnar went greedily from place to place, devouring all she saw. Pawing through the
debris, her boy discovered a drinking horn, and she searched till
she found mead. He placed himself awkwardly on a bench and
began to gulp cup after cup of the honeyed drink. She told him to
stay in the hall, and proceeded alone to the living quarters. Dim
memories of a happier time drew her like a spell.

The raiders must have swept in and out like a summer storm—

here and there bits of treasure still lay about, a brooch, a cloak, a spear. This village had housed only a dozen families, it seemed, but to her—who had not seen a bed or a piece of jewelry in so long—it gleamed with opulence. With sick pleasure she flung a cloak about her shoulders and fastened it with a brooch. A fine lady, she said to herself. A fine lady indeed.

The moon had risen to its height, and when she heard the squeaking sounds of a horn, Ginnar's first thought was that Odin and the Wild Hunt had come for them. Then she realized the trumpeting came from the hall. She ran back to her boy in panic, but there he was, horn in one hand, broken shield in the other, with a battered helmet perched precariously on his massive head. She winced at this hint of the warrior he might have become.

So she told him about the hall, its trappings and celebrations, how its greatness reflected the strength of the people—even if the people were not truly so great.

Her eyes fell upon a tapestry depicting the now-extinct clan's victory in battle. She reached up and ripped it off the wall.

"Like this," she said, showing it to him. "This is a symbol of all that is wrong with these liars You can how they would create the illusion of goodness—weaving spells of protection that cannot shield them from their own evil."

He merely stared.

At last dawn approached, and they began seeking a place to sleep. Ginnar wanted to return to the forest, but her boy insisted on staying in the village. They burrowed finally beneath deep hay in the byre, and she closed her eyes.

She had been asleep only a moment, it seemed, when suddenly her skin began to tingle. Her boy sat, head cocked to one side, listening. "Horses," Ginnar cried. "Run!"

Like demons they burst out of the byre and toward the forest.

Ginnar heard the warriors' shouts as they spotted her. Distant but closing came the pounding hooves of their mounts. She veered to the east and her boy followed in fleeing terror to the fen, where reeds would hide them and horses could not go.

"Did you see it?" she heard a warrior cry. "A monster! A monster wearing the clothing of a human."

Vaguely recognizing that they meant her, Ginnar slogged through mud and water. Deeper into the swamp the terror drove them, till they found their feet could not touch the ground.

Then the water filled her lungs, and Ginnar realized that she could still breathe.

A day passed before they ventured up out of the fen. Shaken, and with the warrior's exclamations of horror still in her mind, she found a mostly clear pool and leaned over to view her reflection. Abruptly, she was jerked back to that moment of shock so long ago, when she crept out of her birthing bed and over to the corner where her babe lay helpless on the floor.

"Monster!" she screamed.

"Monster," she whispered.

Her boy did not know what to make of her.

Ginnar ripped off the cloak and dove deep into the murky darkness of the marsh. She had longed for a discarded bit of civilization to replace what she lost so long ago. But nails and teeth had become claws and fangs. Silky hair was now thick, coarse fur. The dark magic she had used to protect them had obliterated all vestiges of humanity. It could not be restored.

They lived underwater for many moons, exploring their new-found powers of survival in a world humans could never enter. The swamp led eventually to the sea, and they swam with the massive fiends that sank ships and became the villains of tales.

When at last they came up out of the water and returned to

the forest, much of the past had been washed away. The sunlight offended her watery eyes, and her boy could find no joy even in the hunt.

She had summoned wyrd before to guide them on their way, but it had brought them only suffering. Now Ginnar conjured a darker magic, calling on the future to reveal its secrets. With desperation born of injury and want, she poured all her resentment into the incantation. She carved her vengeance in runes on twisted wood. She invoked the black spell to reveal the shape and nature of her destiny once and for all.

There was sunshine, and a gleaming hall appeared. It was not like the hall in the massacred village, or the hall she remembered from home, but a great, shining meadhall of immeasurable glory and beauty. Its vast golden roof glinted in the sun until she thought she would go blind.

Mercifully, the light softened and the hall disappeared, revealing an ancient lake in an unknown forest. Beside it, on a rock, a figure knelt with hands clasped, head down. Ginnar saw that it was a woman. The woman stood, and turned, and it was Freda—but not Freda. She wore the crown and finery of a queen, but it was not in the style of the Helmings. As the woman turned, a flash of scarlet caught Ginnar's mind's eye. At her waist, this Freda not Freda wore a girdle of red and blue on a sea of yellow silk.

A daughter then, Ginnar thought. Her hands clenched and her face burned, livid with revelation.

The vision faded. Her energy spent, Ginnar crawled into the burrow and slept for a day.

When she woke, she called her boy to her. The spell had taken much strength, but she would not waste any time. She gave him the task, made him promise to come back to her, and vowed it would be worth his while. She told him that after this, he would be free to go where he pleased, do what he pleased, roam or stay as he pleased—after he did this one thing for her, who had given her life for him.

He was gone for a long time. She returned to the swamp and stayed deep underwater, lying dormant in the depths so she could bear to be apart from her boy.

After many moons, as though from very far away, she felt him enter the water. She willed her eyes open and peered sluggishly into the murky depths of the fen. A thin, lonely strand of sunlight filtered down through the filth, illuminating her boy's twisted face. She stared dully into his eyes as consciousness returned.

"My Grendel," she said.

He opened his mouth to reveal rows of sharp, deadly teeth.

"I have found it," he growled.

Chapter Seven

"What is it?" I asked, holding the girdle out to Muni.
She sat down on the bench beside the bed and stared at the fabric in my hands. "It's beautiful," she said.

I sat down next to her and she reached out to touch the girdle's braided edge. "Beautiful," she said again.

"Muni," I replied impatiently. "What is this?"

She put her hands in her lap and took a breath.

"When I was chosen to accompany you to Heriot," she began, "your mother the queen came to me with a very important task. She told me many things that were to be revealed when the time was right."

I had never seen the Lady Muni so serious, and said so.

"I took my vow to service solemnly," she agreed. "Your mother the queen is a wise woman, and she made me to understand how important it was."

Clearing her throat, she continued, "The history of this girdle is the greatest secret I've ever kept, or ever hope to keep."

Muni had always been one for dramatic flair, and I was a rapt audience for the story she was about to tell. "Go on," I encouraged her.

"Many years ago," she began, with the cadence of someone who had rehearsed her words well, "there were two young noblewomen who came together to a new land, where one had been chosen to marry the king. Like us," she smiled. I nodded.

"The girl who was not to be queen," Muni said, "was a gifted weaver and seamstress. There was magic in her weaving, and she was of great help to the queen in taking on the new responsibilities.

"A year went by, and the queen did not become with child. Another year went by, and still there were no heirs to the throne, and no expectation of any. Troubled, the queen prayed daily to Freyja, the goddess of fertility, and undertook many rituals to bring about a change. But nothing worked.

"Finally, the weaver determined to create a charm to help her dearest friend. She began work on a girdle that would ensure fertility for the queen.

"With precious silk the king had brought back from the summertime excursions, along with fine wool threads she spun herself, the weaver set about to fashion the girdle.

"For many weeks, the queen watched as her friend sang softly to herself at the loom, working the long days of the summer to create the magical item. As the beautiful fabric began to take shape, the queen found herself awed by her friend's skill and loyalty. The threads themselves fairly shone with quiet hope and anticipated joy.

"When the girdle was finally complete, the weaver presented it to the queen with a blessing of fertility and love. And not a year later, a daughter was born. There was much rejoicing.

"Soon thereafter, the weaver herself became pregnant. The queen was ecstatic that the two friends would be able to raise

their children together. When the time came, the queen her closest companion was there to help. But it was not to be."

"What do you mean?" I asked, alarmed, thinking of my own
lost babe. "You mean the babe died?"

"No," Muni said. "That would have been a blessing. It was a
monster."

"A monster?" I exclaimed.

"The babe was born deformed," she explained, "and its father
would not pick it up." Muni paused for a moment, a frown on
her face.

"The story should have ended there," she said softly. "As is the
custom, it should have been taken to the woods and returned to
the gods and goddesses.

"But this was not to be. While the queen and the husband
were outside, discussing how best to tell the king, the weaver herself picked the child up—"

"No," I interjected.

Muni nodded, her face grim. "And she nursed it."

I was shocked. I had never heard of such an act.

We sat for a moment, eyes fixed on the girdle in my lap. So the weaver had doomed herself to death. Reluctantly, I asked, "And then?"

"Well," Muni said, "the weaver begged the queen, her lifelong
friend, to help her. And so the queen went to her husband the
king. She pleaded for her friend's life, and even for the life of the
cursed child.

"The king was a fair man, and he knew that his wife loved her
friend. But he valued rule and law above matters of the heart, as a
wise king often must. After much reflection, he decreed that the
weaver's life would be spared. But he declared that the babe, the
monster, must die.

"The queen was heartbroken—both by what her friend

had done and by the fact that her friend must now lose her babe. Mindful of all the weaver had done for her, the queen went to her friend in the night and told her what the king had commanded.

"The weaver would have nothing of it. She had suckled, she said, and he was her babe. She would not leave him to die. She begged the queen to help her, reminding her of the girdle, of how she had made it possible for the queen to have her own child.

"The queen knew what her friend had done for her. But she also knew the limits of her own power. It was hers to obey the laws of the people and the dictates of the king. She entreated the weaver to accept it, and to make peace with circumstance.

"When the warriors came to her quarters the next morning, the weaver was gone. Nothing was heard or seen of her again, though the king dispatched his warriors to find her. Her body and the body of her monstrous babe were never found, but it was certain they perished in the wild.

"The queen said a prayer for her dearest friend on that terrible morning, and every morning thereafter for many years, until it became apparent that she would never return."

Muni paused.

"The storyteller himself could not have concocted such a tale," I said after a moment. Holding up the girdle, I asked, "So how did my mother come to have this?"

Muni looked at me strangely, and said, "The queen in this story is your mother. And you are the babe who was brought into the world by this girdle."

I stared at her in amazement.

"It cannot be!" I exclaimed. "It is not possible that such a tale could be true and Mother not tell me. Why would she not tell me?" I was struck by a sudden thought. "I could have used this! I could have used it and my babe would have been saved."

Muni bowed her head at my outburst. "As was told to me by the queen your mother," she said quietly, "the magic works only when it is called. The need must be great—strong enough to invoke the spell."

I pondered this, wrestling with and finally letting go of the notion that my lost babe might somehow have survived.

Muni continued, "Your mother the queen said that wyrd would guide you to find the girdle when the time was right."

"My mother," I replied thoughtfully. I recalled how, on the day we parted, she had said she would be there if I ever needed her. "I saw her at the lake," I told Muni, describing my vision on the water. "And she came to me last night in a dream. She told me to look in the clothes chest."

"Even when you were expecting your babe, I could say nothing," Muni said. "And I longed to help you after it was lost. But the queen your mother was very clear. I could essentially speak of it only if I came into a room and found you holding it, as I have at last."

I took one end of the girdle and Mum took the other. We pulled it taut and held it up between us.

"What was her name?" I asked almost reverently.

"The Lady Ginnar," she said.

I shook my head. "I never heard my mother speak that name. And I have never seen such craft."

Muni murmured agreement. "The magic will work for you now," she told me. "But it will not work for anyone else. You are to recite a verse."

She spoke the spell, and I repeated it. "Desperate desire, waken now the charm. Worn in faith by day, keep my babe from harm."

When the warriors returned a few weeks later, I knew at last what my mother had felt all those years—the nagging worry for a husband's safety that turned gradually to joyful anticipation of reunion. A guard announced their coming, and all of Heorot rushed to convene in the ring of gathering. The jostling assembly spoke in progressively more excited tones, occasionally laughing or practicing a song of welcome.

The company rode up in a cloud of dust, Hrothgar and Esher at the head. Laden with spoils, the weary horses jangled to a halt before the great hall. The crowd cheered and shouted, searching for loved ones and calling to them with delight.

Battle-worn but regal in his bronzed helmet and clanking armor, Hrothgar dismounted and strode toward me. I saw that he was uninjured, and ran to him with excitement and relief.

"Hrothgar!" I exclaimed, casting ceremony aside for once and throwing my arms around him. He returned the embrace, looking down into my face.

"Wealtheow," he said. "Never has my heart been so warmed by a homecoming."

"I thank the goddesses and gods for allowing me to see you again," I said truthfully.

"The sight of you is balm for a hundred battles," Hrothgar replied, lowering his voice and pulling me closer. "It heartens an old king, to be greeted with such fondness."

"And thus may an old king yet have a young heart," I replied happily, taking him by the arm. "Come, let me help you clean up. There's a roadful of dust in your hair." With a stream of cheerful talk that made him smile, I led the king to the baths.

How we feasted that night! In high spirits, Hrothgar handed

out treasure to his warriors and spoke eloquent words of thanks for their courage and loyalty. The storyteller sang fresh tales recounting the latest victories of the Danes.

I was so glad to have Hrothgar safely returned to me, and so newly optimistic about our future, that the world fairly sparkled with possibility. I knew that the king saw the change in me and was slightly perplexed, but gratified.

I pondered whether to tell him about the girdle. In the end, I decided to keep my mother's secret. Some things by their nature belong in the domain of women, and telling my husband now would only distract him from his own responsibilities and concerns.

In a matter of moons, I was pregnant. Hrothgar made the announcement, again, at the Yule celebration. But this time I knew it was different. Even when the telling stone drew forth another dire prediction from the Lady Eir, I remained unconcerned. I had the magic now. Nothing could harm my babe.

Winter passed uneventfully, and when warmer weather came I made my way to the lake as often as I could. I spent hours on its shore, praying to the goddesses and gazing into the calm blue-gray water. Mother did not appear to me again, but I knew that the ancient mere was an essential part of my good fortune. It was a place of safety, and I felt certain its primeval magic would protect my babe and me.

The girdle I kept secured beneath my overdress while I was awake. I often pondered its history, the story of its maker, and my mother. What a secret to keep from me all these years! How tragic the aftermath of such a wondrous charm. With the softening of sensibilities that accompanies being with child, I imagined how I would feel in Ginnar's place. What would I do if my babe were born a monster?

But no. That could not happen. I had the girdle, the magic born of love and desperation. It would protect my babe—I was certain of it.

The spring feast of Ostara passed, as did the anniversary of the loss of my first babe. Hrothgar delayed the summertime excursions to await the birth of the child, sending out scouting troops instead to maintain the roads and explore new routes to the south.

At last, on Midsummer's Day, our daughter was born. She was a healthy, robust little thing, without the slightest sign of weakness or malady.

Hrothgar picked her up proudly and said, "I declare you Freawaru, daughter of Hrothgar and Wealtheow, princess of the Danes."

A few days later, with a prayer of thanks, I packed the girdle away in the bottom of my clothes chest.

As autumn approached, it came time for celebration of another kind. With great feasting and revelry, the Lady Muni was married at last. Her husband, the warrior Wigmund, was a handsome young prince of the Wendel tribe. A man of strong arm and calm eye, the noble warrior's unflappable nature was the perfect companion to Muni's exuberance. It was a well-chosen match.

After her marriage, Muni continued to attend me, but now that she was a wife and I had a babe, we agreed I required another attendant. We had been watching the young ladies of Heorot closely, and after much discussion, Muni and I selected Dagmar, a girl of thirteen, to be my primary helper with little Frea.

"Your Highness honors us with this appointment," her mother

said as she brought the girl before me. "My husband was killed last year in battle, and Freyja knows we have suffered since then, my lady."

"My sympathies to you, Lady Sigrid," I told her. "Your loyalty to the throne of the Danes will certainly be rewarded." To Dagmar, I said, "I welcome you to my service, Lady Dagmar. My babe the princess sleeps at the moment, but when she wakes I will bring you to her."

Dagmar made the formal bow and spoke the proper words of thanks. As she finished speaking, I saw her eyes travel to the loom in the corner.

"Are you a weaver of tapestries?" I asked.

The girl dropped her eyes, embarrassed, but replied softly, "Yes, my lady, though my skill is far from yours." I bowed my head in thanks for her words of praise, picturing the completed tapestry that now hung in the great hall. Even I had been surprised by the results—I had never woven with such inspiration. My love and loyalty for Hrothgar fairly sang out in the vivid colors and delicate forms. The king assured me that his luck had returned, as promised by Odin long ago in the dream.

"As you can see," I said to Dagmar, pointing at the loom, "I am now at work on a second banner for the great hall. I hope to complete it by spring. Perhaps you will be able to assist me."

"I would be honored," the girl said, her face brightening. The Lady Sigrid smiled and I did likewise, feeling good about my choice of helper.

Because her mother was one of Heorot's principal weavers, Dagmar had spent much of her life in the weaving sheds. Lady Sigrid had taught her well, and Dagmar's skill with the loom was wondrous for a girl her age. We passed many hours of the short winter days working on the tapestry together, singing the spells and taking turns weaving when fingers grew tired. Though we each had our own style—as all weavers do—and had been trained in the differing fashions of the Helmings and the Danes, the resulting work was nonetheless excellent in design and technique.

I followed Dagmar sometimes to the sheds, where she went to be with her mother. The Lady Eir was often there as well, sewing and waiting for the cold weather to pass. She had given birth to a babe at Yuletime, a girl she and Esher called Thora in honor of the god. I knew Eir was eager to introduce her babe to the forests and fields where she gathered the healing herbs.

Though she preferred the kitchens, Muni came to the sheds on occasion to chat and sing with the ladies. I would joke with her then about the need to catch up to us and begin having babes, but she seemed content to concentrate on her role as wife to Wigmund.

"Wigmund says there is no rush, that wyrd will provide," Muni said.

"I am surprised you allow him to speak on the subject," I teased her.

"Just as our king is not permitted to refuse a dance," she retorted.

"The king of the Danes loves to dance," I protested.

"If that is so," Eir asked innocently, "then why had I rarely seen him do so before a certain nimble princess came along to 'encourage' him?" The ladies chortled.

"In the queen's defense," said Sigrid, "I am certain I saw the king dance . . . once, I believe, when I was a girl." They laughed again and I joined in with amusement.

These mothers of Heorot, joking and chatting as they sewed or worked the looms, recalled to me the happy days of my childhood. Steadfast wyrd went ever its way, and now I was one of the circle of ladies. Someday soon little Frea would sit at my feet, listening to the stories of our people and learning from the wisdom of her elders.

"I believe you are dancing right now in your mind, Wealtheow," Muni said. Dagmar giggled as I pretended to frown.

"To the contrary, Lady Muni," I said solemnly. "I am contemplating when your Lord Wigmund will again be allowed to express an opinion on children."

The ladies chuckled, and I regarded them fondly. They were an ever-present source of strength and enjoyment in my life. The king had his advisors of the bench, and I had my ladies of the loom.

"I thank Frigga for such a cheerful retinue," I said. Eir nodded her head with a smile, and the others murmured thanks and accord as we set once again to the work at hand.

And so we passed the seasons, which in turn became the years. I approached my fifth winter at Heorot, little Frea now a child of two and I myself nearing twenty. With my babe no longer a babe, I had taken to wearing the girdle again in hopes of having another—this time, perhaps, a son who would grow up to rule the Danes. I knew my daughter's path would eventually lead her far from me, just as my mother and I had followed our wyrd to other parts of the world.

I no longer frequented the lake, but I had vowed to make the proper offerings and prayers of fertility before the season peaked and it became too cold to venture out. I felt certain the girdle itself would provide adequate blessing, but there was no need to take chances.

My only unhappiness was that I still could not feel the trees. In the forest, I would place my hands on their trunks—young saplings, stately elders—but there was no sensation, no hint of the earlier humming warmth. I did not understand how I had lost this connection I so cherished, or how to get it back.

That winter began like all the others, with the great feast of gathering and the warriors' settling into the hall for the season. As I waited in the antechamber for the ceremony to begin, I fingered the soft silk of my sea-blue dress, remembering the first time I had worn it. From wedding day to Gathering to Yule and around the wheel again, I never tired of its beauty, how it flowed when I danced like a wave on the ocean. Coiled silver brooches held the dress at my shoulders, and matching silver armrings spiraled down and around my arms. A necklace of beaten gold lay on the pale skin of my neck, shining in harmony with the crown on my head. I adjusted the golden circlet and smoothed my hair as Hrothgar began the words of welcome. Muni handed me the horn cup, as always, and I entered the main room.

The great hall was ever astonishing in its glory. Light from the immense hearthfire glinted off the precious household treasures of gold, silver, and bronze, and gleamed in the armor and jewelry of the multitude. The tapestry I had woven hung high in a place of honor, its vibrant threads glowing with spells of prosperity.

I approached Hrothgar on his throne and spoke the blessing of the cup. He drank, and I served the mead to each of the royal advisors. Lord Unferth stared impassively ahead as he always did, though after these many years his lack of warmth no longer troubled me. At any rate, it was made up for twofold by the kindly demeanor of the wise Esher, who reminded me so much of my father and often provided me with helpful advice (through Lady Eir). Next I served the boy Hrothulf, now nearly a man but ever my little trickster. Too often was he inclined to wink at me mischievously when he ought to be thinking on his solemn vows to the king.

"Warriors," Hrothgar said. "I welcome you. Winter is upon us, and the time of togetherness is here once again. Today at this feast of the Gathering, and during each day of the season, let us enjoy one another's company, and remember that we are all one people."

The crowd cheered and Hrothgar raised his arm in the air for silence. He continued, "For your service and your loyalty to the throne of the Danes, you have been rewarded with silver and gold. Most important, you have made this hall your home, a refuge that is the pride of the nation. A toast to the Danish kingdom, and to Heorot—the greatest people, and the greatest meadhall, in the world." The multitude shouted in affirmation, and the lively feast began.

We enjoyed a delicious banquet of succulent meats, warm bread, and spicy roasted roots as the storyteller began to sing his songs. He told wondrous tales of heroes and gods, celebrating the people and their faith. Then music filled the hall, sounding to the rafters and accompanied by enthusiastic clapping and stomping of feet. I watched the ladies' dresses swirl as their warriors spun them about.

"My lord," I turned to Hrothgar, suddenly recalling a long-ago conversation with my ladies. "Is it true you never danced before we married?"

The king shifted in his seat, looking slightly uncomfortable. "Who has spoken such treason?" he replied guiltily. I laughed, and he said, "Let us just say, my queen, that I never before recognized the magic of the dance, till I had the pleasure of dancing with you."

"Well spoken." I clapped appreciatively. "The king of the Danes is ever a master of diplomacy."

He nodded and rose from his throne. "To the dance, then," he said, offering his hand with a grin.

If only I had known to treasure that carefree time. Later, I would recall those moments of security and well-being as the ephemeral landscape of a dream—so real in seeming, but gone in an instant.

Chapter Eight

A nd so Ginnar set out with Grendel on their last journey together, to the meadhall of her vision. They traveled across
the plains and through the forests, coming ever closer to populated areas. The air was thick with the smell of humans, and her
disquiet grew. Even in the deep of the woods she could find no
respite. Only when she dove into the darkened depths of some
unfortunate lake was she able to quell her urge to flee.

Despite this discomfort, she knew that traveling to the people
was the only way to find what she sought. Wyrd had shown her
that they would meet their destiny here in the midst of civilization, at the great golden hall of some large triumphant tribe.

As she grew more anxious, her boy seemed to become more
excited. He was ever sniffing the air, cocking his head to listen for
voices or a song on the wind. She was sure he must feel they were
swimming through humans.

He did not ask why they traveled to the hall. He seemed to feel
the pull of it almost as strongly as she did, and that was reason
enough to be going.

As they traveled, he described what he had seen when he

came to the hall the first time. How he had arrived at night and stared at the immense thatched roof shining like silvered gold in the moonlight. How he heard sounds so strange and harsh to his ears that he had to retreat further from the mead-hall to be able to endure it. How the storyteller sang of the people's greatness.

The humans never suspected he was there, even when he drew near—so close that he could almost taste their scent as it grew palpable on the air. He could hear the poet's every word. He learned the name of the hall and the king who ruled it. They were a nation founded by a foundling, the orphan Shield Sheafing, whose strength and determination were born again in the fierce and wise King Hrothgar. The Danish kingdom's glory culminated in Heorot, the greatest meadhall in the world.

Ginnar seemed to recall Hrothgar's name, but it was lost in the recesses of unneeded memory. The harshness of the wilderness had scrubbed her mind clean of such unimportant details. Sometimes she found that she could not even remember her own name.

Occasionally over the years, especially as she was falling asleep or upon waking, Ginnar would recollect the reassuring, tactile pleasures of her old life—a certain scent, the touch of a hand, the sound of a friendly voice. But her boy's birth day loomed above these small slivers of the past like a hammer, pounding them out of recollection. All she needed to know was that she and her boy had been cast out—condemned to death by those who claimed to love them.

So what then of the second image in her vision, the Freda not Freda at an ancient mere? This was not the land of the Helmings. "And the queen?" she asked him.

"Wal—Wallchow," he pronounced with difficulty.

"Wealtheow?" she said faintly, though she already knew it was her. He grunted, then, tired of talk, lifted his nose into the air and loped off on the trail of their dinner.

Freda's daughter had been sold to make peace. The vision swam before her, this Freda not Freda wearing the girdle Ginnar had woven—magic created in love, then bitterly betrayed. Her nailclaws dug into the palms of her hands and she clenched her teeth with anger.

It was not peace the princess would bring her adopted clan now.

After an eternity of travel they drew near the hall. She felt it like Thor's thunderbolt, the constant rising of hair on her neck and the painful prickling of skin. Finally, she stopped and could go no further. Her boy urged her on, but she could not bring herself to approach the hall.

Instead, she led him into the forest and stood still in the dark, listening to the ancient trees. Then they ran until the wood grew older, deeper. Emerging from the shadow of the forest, they came to a clearing at the shore of a primeval lake. She felt a baleful satisfaction. They had found it—the mere of her vision, a fount of fertility and success.

Its magic was ancient and pure. But it could not keep them out.

The moment they entered the water, the mere began to change. Its clear depths roiled and grew murky. The wind began to blow, stirring up black waves. A foul mist rolled across the surface, and a fearsome heat rose off it.

They dove deep to the muddy bottom, following their noses to an underwater burial chamber. Its maze of rooms bulged with age-old bones. This dismal cavern of death would suit them well.

Soon other creatures joined them, sea beasts with giant jaws and wild eyes, strangely scaled serpents, fiends of darkness Ginnar had never seen. The lake burned at night like a torch, and bubbled with grisly debris during the day.

Deer no longer came to drink at the shore. Trees shrank away, and those with roots in the water began to wither. Their dead branches hung like skeletons over the murky tarn.

Ginnar settled at the bottom of the lake and sent Grendel to the meadhall, warning him to be certain he was not perceived.

When he returned, her boy was agitated and confused. He recounted the tale of the storyteller, the singing which grated and yet compelled him to listen. It was the story of the building of Heorot. The poet told how the great Hrothgar had carved a kingdom from disorder, conquered chaos to bring peace to the nation. How he had built the greatest meadhall on earth, a citadel whose glory could never dim. How the people had risen from nothingness to master their world.

Why must they continually revel in their own glory? Her boy was curious, inquiring as he hadn't for a long time. He noted that after the storytelling and raucousness, the people fell deeply silent, more hushed than the forest at midnight. How could they sleep so peacefully? He couldn't understand their confidence in their own safety. Ginnar answered him tersely, impatient to appease the rising flood of her bitterness.

And to somehow find release for the growing intensity in her boy. He fairly bristled with the need to act, as though his unguided energy might burst out of him at any moment. She could see it when he spoke of the stories.

When the moon orbed high in the sky, she said to Grendel, "The time has come for you to prove the people wrong."

He looked at her, alert and interested in this new thought.

"You alone have the power to show them that their hall can

be conquered," she said. "You come so close to them, yet they cannot perceive you. They imagine themselves secure, but that is illusion."

Her boy did not understand.

"It would be the easiest of tasks for you to slip in and show them how vulnerable they are," she explained. "Rip down their tapestries of protection, ruin their beautiful hall." To herself, she finished the thought: Make them feel the fear and pain I have known at their hands.

Ginnar watched the idea enter and blossom in her boy's mind. He would have to overcome a lifetime of avoidance to carry out her plan. But the tide in him was strong. She knew the desire to act would overrule hesitation.

"I will do it," he said.

She grinned into his wild eyes and warned him to be careful.

"Fly in and out like the wind," she screeched as he set off for the hall. "Don't let them catch you."

She waited for her boy all night, both worried for his safety and anticipating his success. In the darkness before dawn, she felt him coming and hurried to the surface of the lake. To her surprise, he was covered in gore, though she saw with relief that it was not his own. An astounding array of broken bodies formed a trail behind him as he came galloping up to her.

"You killed them," she said in wonder. "And so many."

He grinned a bloody grin. "There were more," he growled, "but I dropped some in the woods. And ate others."

Ginnar had never seen him so satisfied.

He recounted how it had happened. When the revelers fell into their deep silence, he had slunk up to the hall, slipping through the great doors undetected.

In the light of the fire, he saw the tapestry on the wall where she had said it would be. With a muted growl, he ripped it down and threw it into the flames. The light flared, and his eyes fell on the senseless warriors around him, deep in sleep and anticipating no danger. Oh, their inadequate senses!

He was dizzied by their nearness, the quiet roar of their breathing, the overwhelming odor. He reached down silently toward the closest warrior, fingers itching to touch the exposed skin, and plucked the human up. To his surprise, he discovered he had crushed its skull.

Amazed by the ease of it, surprised at their fragility, he grabbed up another and, on impulse, bit into the soft flesh. Suddenly drunk on the bloody power of it, the brilliant explosion of excitement, he snatched them up by the dozens, running and chomping all the way back to Ginnar.

"The humans didn't even know I was there," he said gleefully. "Perhaps they will not discover my triumph until the sun rises."

"And then they will come for you," Ginnar said, alarmed for a moment. "You have led them here with the blood of their own warriors."

"Let them come," Grendel replied, eyes shining fiercely. "What can they do? I am as powerful as the gods in your stories, Mother."

She looked at him and knew it was true. But he was more like a giant than a god. His twisted face and hungry eyes spoke of realized power and future havoc.

"They are weak," Grendel growled, "weaker than babes." He shook the limb in his hand for emphasis, and a fine spray of blood flew through the air between them. "I can do as I please." He spat the words like venom.

Ginnar grinned, realizing that at long last, it was done—she had her recompense, lives taken in payment for the lives stolen from them long ago.

And her boy had found his purpose.

As Grendel continued to revel in his spoils, Ginnar turned away and gazed at the moonlight on the lake. Its mystic rays worked feebly to drive the madness from the mere, but it could bring only the slightest shimmer to the wounded surface. She raised her face to its futile light and howled with feral abandon. After a moment, Grendel joined her, baying all other sound to silence. When they stopped, she could hear only the gentle drip, drip, dripping of life from the ragged remains in her boy's hands.

Wyrd had brought them only suffering, but they had risen above it at last. We have stepped outside the stream, she thought. No longer would empty fate choose their course. There would be no more misery for them at human hands.

"We have become more than wyrd would have us be," she said to her boy, who glanced up from his meal but did not stop chewing. She smiled at him fondly. "Now we will be their destruction."

Chapter Nine

We went to sleep that night with peaceful hearts and easy minds. When we woke, our lives as we knew them had ended, and a nightmare had begun.

The cries of the warriors roused me, and I rushed to the great hall with my attendants scrambling in tow. Women ahead of me began to wail. I ran through the antechamber and into the main room.

Hrothgar stood by the great fire, a burned fragment of tapestry in his hand. At his feet lay the mangled bodies of several warriors. Esher and Unferth stood with him, and I saw them look toward the far doors.

As I struggled through the chaos of shouting warriors and keening women to reach the king, Muni ran up to me in a panic.

"I cannot find Wigmund," she cried. "I cannot find him anywhere." I took her hand and together we made our way to Hrothgar, Esher, and Unferth. They stood staring at the ground. I followed their eyes, and saw a grisly trail of blood leading from the hall.

"What happened?" I cried. Unferth glared at me, but the king permitted my intrusion and looked up from the bloody tracks.

"Murder," he said. "Whether men or beasts, we don't yet know." He turned and strode from the great hall, following the trail of blood out the doors and to the south. Muni and I staggered along behind him, stunned and then horrified as we came upon a warrior's limb at the edge of the village.

"Where is Wigmund?" Muni shrieked.

Hrothgar stopped and turned to the group of warriors who had followed him out of the hall. "We ride to find and kill the invaders," he announced. "I will have the bravest warriors of Heorot accompany me." Calling a dozen of them by name, he chose a contingent and then spoke to Esher in quiet tones.

"I would have you remain here, my friend," he said. "Hrothulf will have need of your wise counsel should I not return."

My breath caught in my throat and I stifled a sob. Muni was crying uncontrollably. "We were waiting to have babes," she sobbed.

Eir ran up to us, her relieved eyes falling on her husband.

"Take Muni back to her quarters," I said. She nodded, exchanging a glance with Esher.

"We were waiting to have babes," Muni repeated as they walked away.

"I should also remain, my lord," Unferth said suddenly. "It would not do for the Danes to lose the best of their leaders and advisors."

"So you expect defeat rather than crave victory, Lord Unferth," I snapped at him. Hrothgar raised his hand in the air.

"Peace," he said, and to Unferth, "So be it. Prepare my horse, then." To the larger group, he declared, "We meet here as soon as we are ready. Those who have dared offend the Danes will meet their doom today."

I followed Hrothgar back to the king's quarters and, shooing off his servants, brought him nourishment. "Do you think the Lord Wigmund is dead?" I asked as he shoveled the food thoughtlessly into his mouth.

He looked at me grimly. Deep lines I had never seen appeared around his mouth and forehead. He stared at me for a moment, seeing but not truly seeing, then took a swig of mead and shook his head.

"Six are dead," he said, wiping his mouth on his sleeve, "and two dozen missing. The killers of my warriors were brutal in their actions, and I have no reason to expect survivors. But we won't know until we find them whether the missing are dead or alive."

I nodded, then helped him prepare the war gear and don the shining armor.

At the edge of the forest, the warriors sat astride their eagerly shifting mounts, faces stern beneath majestic helmets. Their gleaming swords hung at the ready, and their sharp-tipped spears shone with anticipation of retribution.

Hrothgar looked down at me from his gilded horse. He reached out his hand, and I took it.

"May victory be yours," I said, repeating the traditional battle prayer. "And may you return to me, my king, in triumph over the evil marauders who have dared to assail the great hall."

He nodded, then wheeled toward the forest and galloped into the wood. The fearsome contingent followed with shouts of vengeance. The last warrior into the forest carried the banner of the Danes, its red and black emblem snarling fiercely from the cloth.

As they rode away, clouds covered the sun, and I shivered with cold and fear.

All morning we waited in horrible expectation. Eir and I sat with Muni as she first wailed then spoke then sobbed her sorrow. We could do nothing to comfort her. "We were waiting to have babes," she said over and over again.

Meanwhile, servants piled high a funeral pyre of wood and brush. The bodies of those who had been killed were placed on top along with their battle gear. Grief-ridden wives and children sat beside the pyre in wailing watch. Warriors sang mournful dirges of loss and waited to see whether there would be additions to the pile.

When the sun was high in the sky, we heard shouts and ran to the ring of gathering. "Make way for the queen," an attendant called as I hurried through the jostling crowd.

Hrothgar came into view and my heart beat again.

Then I saw he was alone.

No other warrior came cantering up behind. He rode, solitary, through the crowd to the door of the great hall. He was covered in blood, and holding his arm as though injured. "I will have my advisors to me," he shouted, dismounting and hastening into the hall. Guards at the door would admit no one else. I craned my neck to see inside as the advisors entered and the great doors slammed shut.

The people waited outside the hall in the ring of gathering, anxious to know what was happening and filled with rising fear. I sent for Eir and she joined me after a few moments, carrying her healer's bag.

"Hrothgar is hurt," I said.

"I will tend to him when their meeting is finished," she reassured me, putting her arm around my shoulder. I felt the tears well but brushed them back angrily. Compelled by my feeling of helplessness, I ordered the kitchen workers to begin preparing the evening's repast. I had the guards send the children and their caregivers away. Around me the agitated crowd debated the reasons for the attack.

"The wild tribes of the South must have eluded our border guard," an old warrior asserted.

"It seems more the work of animals," replied a young man. "A pack of wolves gone mad."

"Wyrd is punishing us," rejoined the woman beside him. "This is a curse for wrongdoing."

At last the great doors opened and Esher came out into the ring.

"Our warriors have been killed," he said with pain. A great wailing rose from the crowd. Wives and mothers cried out in anguish.

He continued bleakly, "There will be no more bodies for the pyre. A foul creature of the deep has destroyed all remains of our brave warriors, leaving only the king of the Danes to return to Heorot."

He gazed out at the people sorrowfully, and said, "Let us burn our dead, that they may make the final journey to Valhalla, where they feast forever with the gods."

The guards would let no one near, but Eir and I called to Esher and he waved us in.

We rushed through the hall to the dais where Hrothgar sat. He lay back in his throne wearily, blankly, like a man who moves in his sleep. I knelt before him, barely able to keep the trembling out of my voice.

"My lord," I said. "The Lady Eir would tend your wounds."

"So be it," he muttered, and Eir moved to examine him.

"The repast is prepared," I said to Unferth, who stood beside the dais. He nodded and called to a guard.

"Make it known," he told the guard, "that the people will eat, for the throne of the Danes provides. But there will be only mourning tonight." The guard saluted and moved out to spread the word.

"The bone is not broken, but this wound will take some time to heal," Eir said as she began to wrap Hrothgar's arm. He winced in pain, then looked over to Esher and Unferth.

"We regroup tomorrow at daybreak," he said. "Preside over the repast. My wounds have made me weary. Wealtheow, attend me."

I rose quickly and accompanied him to the king's quarters, stealing glances at his exhausted face as we made our way from the hall. Guards kept the people away, but Hrothgar called to them, "Courage. We regroup tomorrow."

His shoulders sagged as we entered the room, and he collapsed on the bed. I ran to him.

"Hrothgar!" I exclaimed. He shook his head at me.

"I am fine. Tired. That's all."

I sat down beside him and put my hand on his face. He closed his eyes and leaned into it with a sigh.

"What happened?" I asked softly.

When he opened his eyes, the desperate expression in them shocked me with fear.

In a voice filled with anger and despair, he recounted the contingent's trek through the forest, following the trail of blood and gore. Several times they came to the carnage of their fallen comrades. It became clear that they were not in pursuit of men, but monsters.

"Monsters!" I exclaimed.

"The bodies were ripped apart," he said bluntly. "No human could have done it. No animal could carry so many."

At last they had come to the end of the trail, to a lake in the ancient forest. The water bubbled black with blood, and hideous serpents undulated through the filth, their strangely scaled coils writhing above the surface and then disappearing beneath.

They had sat on their nervous horses for a moment, searching the scene for any trace of the disappeared warriors. But there was nothing, and it seemed that their fellows had been taken straight into the cursed lake. Of the enemy there was no sign. The warriors made their way around the shore of the lake, leaving their anxious mounts at the tree line and carrying their great battle swords at the ready.

Suddenly there was a splash, and two of the warriors disappeared into the black water. Others rushed to their aid, only to be dragged under by some unseen force. Hrothgar and the remaining warriors formed a quick phalanx and made their way to the spot where the others had vanished.

And then there rose from the malevolent mere a hideous creature the likes of which Hrothgar had never seen. Like a giant, evil and supreme, it grabbed his warriors up and smashed them into the ground before Hrothgar could even swing his sword. Bodies flew, and the king was flung against a rock at the edge of the poisonous water. His arm gouged by twisted, tainted roots, he struggled to rise, certain of death but determined to die in battle with the creature who killed his men.

"But when I rose," he said, "the monster had vanished. I made my way finally to the forest, where I was blessed to find my mount. All my warriors, and their horses, were gone."

"Oh, Hrothgar," I said, horrified.

"I would have destroyed it. Odin knows I tried. Now my finest warriors are dead," he said in agony.

We sat bowed in silence for a long while. A servant brought us the meal, and I checked quickly on little Frea, who had been in Dagmar's care all day. When I returned, I asked Hrothgar a question that had been growing in my mind since he recounted the ill-fated excursion.

"This lake," I said reluctantly. "Where was it?"

He told me, and I knew. It was my lake. The lake where Mother had come to me, the lake that had helped me have my babe. Now tainted, cursed, filthy with horror and death.

Hrothgar lay down to sleep, and I retired to my own quarters. As I walked from his rooms, I watched the sun set with numb horror.

"What evil has come upon us?" I whispered to the sky.

That night, in the depths of darkness, the monster returned to Heorot, and had its way with our lives.

Chapter Ten

Ginnar watched her boy swim through the entrance of their lair, hands full of body parts. The humans had put up such a feeble, futile fight. There was no comparing her boy's might to theirs.

Her eyes glowed from the dark corner where she sat hunched, arms wrapped around knotted legs, and Grendel spotted her at once. His expression altered quickly from glee to a subtle sullenness.

"Why did I have to let him live?" he asked impatiently. "I wanted to kill them all."

"He will suffer more to survive," Ginnar said. *And the queen,* she thought. *She will suffer at his side.*

Her boy regarded her appraisingly. "We are more alike than I thought, Mother," he said at last. She laughed, a guttural cough of mirthless air.

When he had slept and the day was waning, her boy came to her with action in his eyes. "I will return tonight," he said, "and do the same."

"They will be expecting you," she pointed out.

"Even so, they cannot stop me," he sneered, obviously proud of his newfound power.

"They have magic," Ginnar said distantly, though she knew a day was not enough to conjure a spell that could threaten her boy. If a resistant charm were possible at all, it would take years of intense spell weaving by gifted casters to counter the lifetime of protection she had placed on him.

Grendel shook his head disparagingly. "I am free now," he said. "Free even of wyrd. And remember your words—I can do as I please."

It was true, she had promised him freedom in exchange for leading them to Heorot. But she would not leave her son. Her Grendel, who had never controlled anything, not even his own existence, now had more power and importance than Ginnar could ever have hoped. There was no telling how long he would amuse himself with his domination of the humans. He had found his calling in enacting her revenge.

As Ginnar had watched her boy sleep, however, she discovered that the craving for vengeance had not ebbed. His triumph should have satisfied, but the hateful hunger still gnawed.

"Do one thing," she said, an idea coming to her. "Don't touch the throneseats. Destroy what you will, but leave those unharmed. They will be a constant reminder of the king's inability to protect his people."

Grendel nodded and turned away.

"I am going to rest," she called after him, suddenly weary. "Call if you need me."

He did not reply.

Entering the underwater tunnels that lay deep in the recesses of their lair, Ginnar wandered aimlessly for a while. She had thought recompense would ease the painful, ever-present emptiness. Perhaps no amount of human suffering would be enough.

Eventually she came to a small grotto just large enough for her body. Climbing inside, she curled up in the jagged space. Her eyes closed, and she felt her breathing slow into hibernation. Sleep could halt the gnawing, and her boy could provide for himself. He would sustain his life by taking others'. It was as it should be, Ginnar thought hazily as she drifted to sleep. After all, they had taken his life from him.

Chapter Eleven

Like a nightmare repeating itself, the day began with anguished cries. Again, I rushed to the great hall, and again, the bodies of the murdered lay in grisly disarray. Hrothgar gave orders to clear the room, and guards ushered the keening women and shouting warriors outside.

"We must secure this hall," Hrothgar said wearily. "We need new iron for the doors. We will keep this monster out." He turned to his advisors. "Esher, assemble the building crew. Unferth, go to the smithy and have them create the new securings." His counselors made the formal bow and went to their business.

I looked around the great hall in silence. Its once spotless glory was now besmirched with blood and violence. So many brave warriors lost. My hope-woven tapestry destroyed. The giant fire growing cold.

"Wealtheow," Hrothgar said, making me jump. I turned to him quickly.

"Yes, my lord?"

"I would have you speak with the Lady Eir. My wound is festering and I could benefit from her attention."

I hurried to him, alarmed, and put my hand on his forehead. "You are feverish," I said. "I will bring her."

I found Eir and Muni in the weaving sheds talking with Sigrid. When she turned to me, Muni's red-rimmed eyes and sorrow-filled face made me want to cry. Instead, I said to Eir, "The king's wound is festering and he asks for you. He is in the hall."

We returned to Heorot in silence.

After examining Hrothgar's arm, which appeared infected—it seemed by the tainted roots at the ill-fated lake—Eir said, "I must have fresh plants from the forest."

"Take a guard," Hrothgar said. Eir nodded and left.

"The women are speaking of spells," I told the king.

"Good," he replied. "Go to them, and tell them what I have told you of the lake. The magic that will defeat this evil must be strong and wise." I hesitated, and he said, "Do not worry for me, Wealtheow. Go do what you must to protect our home, and I will do the same."

"Yes, my lord," I replied, bowing.

In the sheds, Muni and Sigrid sat in conference with some of the other ladies. Joining them, I sat down next to Muni and took her hand. Our eyes met, and with grim purpose I told them of Hrothgar's encounter at the lake.

"Is this a water demon, then?" Muni asked.

"I don't think so, at least not entirely," I replied. "This monster wants to kill our warriors in our hall. Right now the blacksmith is forging new bolts for the door, and the builders are constructing reinforcements."

"We must create a spell of strength for the doors," Sigrid said. The ladies nodded and I rose.

"I will get Eir," I said. "We will need her for the spell weaving." As I left the sheds, I saw the healer coming toward me on the path.

"How is he?" I asked.

"The salve will help," she replied. "But the king needs rest that I fear he can ill afford."

"We are weaving a spell of strength for the doors," I said. "I came to get you."

"I'll come," she said, "but first I must go to the pyre. My cousin Eadwacer was among those killed."

I nodded. "I have been to his wife this morning." It was my duty to attend families of the dead, offering them consolation and reassurance of their continued place in the clan. Eadwacer's children were fortunate that they had uncles to take them in, I had reminded his tearful widow. It seemed small comfort for the little ones huddling silently at their mother's feet.

I gave my friend a sympathetic embrace. "I should have spoken to you as well, Eir. I am sorry."

She shrugged pragmatically, her face drawn. "Many have lost loved ones," she said. "We are lucky his body is here to be burned."

It was the second pyre in two days. Watching the fire burn, I felt that Heorot itself was going up in flames. Why was this demon of the night so intent on killing our people?

By nightfall, the new iron bolts had been fixed on the great doors, and the women had spoken their spells. A cadre of warriors waited in the hall, defiant and courageous.

When morning came, the doors were broken and our warriors were dead.

As the king approached the entrance, wives, sisters, and daughters rushed past him into the hall, throwing themselves onto the mutilated corpses. They wailed their agony in an intolerable chorus of pain. Our spells had failed. Our families were decimated. I stood blankly beside the throne for several moments, staring, till Eir approached and urged me to help her remove the grieving women from the hall.

Hrothgar sent a messenger at once to Kylfa, the chieftain of the Danish Clan of the Spear, requesting their warriors' assistance. He ordered an even stronger framework of iron constructed, along with new wood for the violated doors.

"We will protect our hall," he told me later as I changed the dressing on his arm. I nodded silently, picturing the women weeping over the bodies of their murdered husbands and sons.

"No cursed creature of the night will make himself our master," he continued doggedly. "Kylfa will come with his warriors, and if the doors do not hold, then the monster will breathe its last at the end of a Danish spear."

Night came, and Heorot lay empty. No remaining warrior dared risk his life by staying. Those without quarters or family would sooner sleep in the byre with the animals than spend the night in the afflicted hall.

Eir, Muni, Sigrid, and a fourth weaver—the Lady Disa—undertook to build a more powerful spell for the new doors. For days they sat solemnly around the sacred fire, casting in herbs and building the enchantment. I parceled out my time among the spell casters, the families of the dead, and the kitchens, where the disheartened workers required encouragement to continue their labors. A great number of families were in mourning, and forced in their grief to do the household jobs and community chores their loved ones had once performed. The weaving sheds lay nearly idle.

At last Kylfa's warriors arrived. They had heard about the

monster's acts of terror and were eager to eliminate this destroyer of the Danes.

"My old comrade," Hrothgar said to the chieftain after I had offered around the cup and taken my place beside him. "You come to us in troubled times, and we are grateful for your swords."

"The Danish people are mighty," Kylfa answered. "And their great hall must be defended. We will lie in wait for this monster, and my warriors will end this horrible rampage."

When the builders had finished installing the stronger doors, the women gathered solemnly to cast their carefully woven spell. At dusk, the warriors of Kylfa retired to Heorot, their gleaming swords drawn in anticipation. The well-wrought armor of the Spear Danes shone in the firelight of the great hall.

When morning came, the lone survivor described how the blades of their ancestral swords had glanced off the demon's hide—how proudly the warriors had died, throwing themselves upon the monster as it ate their brothers. The warrior who told this tale had fled as the mouse flees the eagle. Only the cowards are left to us now, I found myself thinking. All our brave warriors are dead.

I knew that Hrothgar longed to defend his hall. But he was injured, and even uninjured he was no longer the warrior hero of his youth. After Kylfa's warriors were killed, the king did not call on the chieftains again. He was heartsick and unwilling to yield more Danes to the monster's pleasure.

And so the once happy hall fell perpetually silent and grim. During the day, we gathered somberly under its vast roof for the business of the people. At night, even the most mundane objects in the hall—bowl, broom, bench—were destroyed by the hateful trespasser. Fortunately, there seemed some small hope: the throneseats themselves remained unassaulted and pristine thanks to the Allfather's protection of the king.

Just as the marauding killer now controlled Heorot, so too did it reign over the plains and paths of the surrounding countryside. Like Odin on the Wild Hunt, the monster sought ever to snatch the people up. Any warrior traveling by night was hunted as he himself might hunt the boar—stalked, stabbed, and eaten.

We prayed daily to the gods and goddesses, begging them to stop what the people could not. Sacrifices were made, and some Danes began worshiping the spirits of the past—ancient beings whose greatest power lay in their dark cruelty. After much deliberation, Eir was even ordered to carve runes into rock. We set these magic stones by the throne of Heorot day after day. Each morning would find them smashed to dust.

New warriors arrived to destroy the monster, coming not at Hrothgar's bidding, but seeking their own fortune. A ragged band of outlaws from the sea, they were welcomed nonetheless and thanked for their courage and valor. Hrothgar promised them treasure and high repute if they succeeded in ridding Heorot of its cruel intruder.

Eir, with young Disa assisting, had been working on a potion that would prove fatal to the monster. She was concerned that it might also harm these warriors, though this was a necessary risk. We bid them smear it carefully on their armor and weapons, but not to let it touch their skin. Those who did would die.

They all died anyway.

In time we came to know that the dark creature lived in the hall by night. This dreadful invasion sapped Hrothgar's strength as no physical wound ever could. It was pain enough that the monster killed wantonly, took life and would not negotiate for peace or pay the blood price. But to know, night after night, that this demon inhabited the great hall as though it were a beastly lair—it was beyond imagining, and yet it was real. Splendid Heorot, the glory of the Danes, had become a mockery of its proud builders. It stood a monument to our humiliation and suffering.

Chapter Twelve

And so the monster ruled by night, and Hrothgar ruled by day.

I hated to see what it did to my husband, this grievous insult to the people that he could not resolve. Though the wound on his arm had begun to heal, the deeper injury robbed him of his confidence and twisted his hope into despair. He sat on the throne day after day, presiding as ever over the business of the Danes, but his shoulders bore the burden of his heart, and the shadow of sorrow was ever on his face.

"My lord," I came to him after a long afternoon, and sat by his side in my throneseat. "Take heart. Our situation must improve. We will find a way to defeat the monster." Even as I spoke the hopeful words, I knew this was a promise easily made but hard to keep.

"I am old, Wealtheow," Hrothgar replied heavily. "What's left of my warriors are barely men. I am three times their age and of half their strength. My advisors and I might form strategy after well-wrought strategy, but we lack the power to execute our plans."

"We must believe that wyrd will provide," I protested gently. "This cannot continue. The way will become clear."

"It is wyrd that brought the monster to us," he said with resignation.

Winter passed into tortured spring, and spring to joyless summer. Our warriors seemed relieved when time came for the excursions. They must have felt blessed to be able to escape our bleak state, if only for a few moons.

For the first time, young Hrothulf would be accompanying the contingent. He had come of age at last and was eager to embark on his first expedition. The rituals to admit him to the warriors' ranks were made grim by our situation, but we carried them out with ceremony nevertheless. He was presented with the traditional spear and shield, and Hrothgar swore him to allegiance in battle.

On my way to speak with Hrothgar, I came upon our nephew the day after the rites, practicing his spear thrusts on a warrior's dummy filled with straw. When he saw me, he straightened proudly and tightened his grip on the spear. I stifled a smile and nodded seriously at his new weapon.

"How is it with your warrior's spear?" I asked. He grinned and thrust it toward me playfully. I resisted the urge to jump back.

"Observe the blade," he said with enthusiasm. "I honed it all night. No spear in the kingdom can match this point." He made a few feints, new shield grasped firmly in the other hand.

"Quite fierce," I agreed. Just then, the Lady Disa passed us on her way to Eir's quarters. Though only fourteen, she was skilled with spell songs, and had been Eir's first choice when another caster was needed to help build the spells for the doors.

Seeing her, Hrothulf paused and puffed his chest out importantly.

"Greetings, Lady Disa," he said.

Disa stopped and made the formal bow. "My lord," she replied.

"Do you know," Hrothulf boasted, "that I will be going to battle this summer?" I held my tongue, resisting the urge to dampen his old proclivity for bragging.

Disa did not appear impressed. "I have heard this," she said. "But surely my lord intends to sing of his accomplishments after he has accomplished them, not before." Hrothulf's countenance fell, and Disa continued down the path.

We watched her depart in silence, and I glanced at Hrothulf sympathetically. Like all our warriors, he would benefit from the excursions. And despite her tartness, Lady Disa's behavior had been proper. It was against the laws of our people to court or be courted. The only suitable way for two people to be together was through marriage arranged by parents or king.

Despite Hrothulf's interest, it was an association that would most likely come to nothing. Because he was the king's nephew, selection of Hrothulf's partner would be of great strategic and political import. The Lady Disa did not figure into that accounting—a fact which seemed to suit her.

I saw Disa and Dagmar together sometimes, whispering to each other in a corner while little Frea played. Their friendship brought to mind Muni and myself at that age. How innocent we had been. The life ahead of us had seemed more dream than reality. It was a time of confidences and joyful anticipation of the future—before we grew up, got married, had a child or lost a husband . . . before the monster came.

I recalled what Mother had often told me. "A queen must have courage and determination," she said, "even in the face of grave danger." I could not imagine what she meant then, when my greatest challenges were a boring task or a difficult ritual to memorize.

Now I was facing the gravest danger of my life, and there was nothing I could do. No matter how courageous or determined I might be, the monster continued to dominate the Danes. Like Hrothgar, I found myself questioning the wyrd that had brought us here.

But it was as Mother had said. We must do what we can, for we cannot avoid our fate. For the sake of the people . . . for the sake of our children, it was our duty to persevere.

I sighed and Hrothulf looked at me sharply. I smiled a reassurance I did not feel and patted his arm.

"I must go speak with your uncle," I said. He bowed and resumed his spear practice with renewed energy. I wondered if he was thinking of Disa.

A servant announced me and I entered the king's quarters, heart beating fast.

"Wealtheow," he rose to greet me.

"Hrothgar," I said at once, taking the proffered hand. "I am with child."

Winter followed winter as we suffered under the monster's cruel oppression. For some, it was a lifetime.

We had lost much as a people. Nearly every family in Heorot was robbed of a father, a son, a brother, an uncle. The workload for survivors increased, while their ability to do the work diminished. I lost count of how many times I came upon a woman weeping beside her weaving or sobbing over an empty washpot.

With no secure gathering place, we also faltered in our efforts to maintain unity. At first we had worked together to repel the creature, but as time went on and our attempts continued to fail, we who had prided ourselves on our hospitality and generosity became wary and suspicious. The meals and celebrations that were so important to our community were shared less frequently. Families kept to themselves, and friendships suffered as competition increased for our dwindling resources. The siege challenged not just our physical survival, but our emotional endurance as well.

Most peculiar about the monster was that it did not inhabit Heorot during the summertime excursions, when the warriors were absent. Each summer gave us the opportunity to rebuild—if not the great hall, then at least some of our spirit. Like that of the untouched throneseats, the people attributed this mystery to the gods' protection. But the simplicity of this explanation bothered me, and I often discussed it with Eir and Muni. What was it about the excursions and the throne that held the monster in check? Why not continue to attack and destroy us once and for all? It was almost as though the creature wanted the Danes to suffer, bringing us again and again to the edge of annihilation only to offer a mocking reprieve each time our warriors took to battle.

Hrothgar and his advisors did not waste much time questioning the monster's actions. They were merely glad to maintain for that short part of the year some semblance of their former lives. The women and children were likewise temporarily free to focus on the comfortingly normal tasks of maintaining crops, restocking foodstores, and weaving clothing and textiles. Without these brief respites, the Danish kingdom would certainly have ceased to exist.

Victory in battle buoyed our warriors, but no matter how many enemy soldiers they conquered, the king and his retinue were powerless to defeat the monster at home. Somehow the creature always knew when they had returned, and its detestable reign would begin again each fall.

I hated to think of it watching us in the night.

Yet amid so much death, life persevered. Hrothgar and I joyfully welcomed two sons to our family. Gentle Hrethric, heir to the throne of the Danes, came along less than a year after the attacks began. And Hrothmund, the very image of his cousin Hrothulf—charming, good-natured, and boastful—followed a few winters later.

Muni remarried and had a daughter of her own, a spirited child called Ingrid. I saw my best friend's darling as the future queen of the Danes, though this honor would certainly go to the princess of some distant tribe.

Eir and Esher's three girls were on their way to becoming healers every bit as skilled as their mother. Even the youngest, at a mere four years old, could diagnose minor ailments and recommend the proper herbs. Just like Eir, all three preferred time in the forest to time spent under a roof.

I often wondered what it would be like for our children to know the way of life that had once been ours. The adults remembered fondly, brokenly, the old days, but our sons and daughters understood only the present onerous existence. What was cruel to us was to them merely the way of life.

This was brought home to me one day when we were in the hall finishing the midday meal. The repast was our largest now that we could not inhabit Heorot at night.

The children were playing at wrestling, with little Hrothmund determined to win. In an attempt to intimidate his opponent, my son bared his teeth and formed his hands into claws. "Roar!" he exclaimed. "I am the monster."

I observed this innocent playacting with horror. "Stop it!" I snapped, rising out of my throneseat. The boys turned to look at me, surprised. I waved them out of the hall and sat back down with a sigh.

"They do not understand," Hrothgar said beside me. I nodded and took his hand.

The many years of siege had aged the king of the Danes. While still highly regarded—there was no more respected ruler in the world—he was stooped and weary of both body and mind. He came to me often in the evenings, even sleeping in my quarters upon occasion. On these nights I would talk to him of our children, telling funny stories about their mishaps and relating small accomplishments. Sometimes, too, I would sing songs or recount his favorite stories—tales of heroes triumphant in battle. Though I sought to remain cheerful, it saddened me to see my husband so diminished.

One of Hrothgar's few pleasures was watching me work the loom, and being surrounded by my tapestries seemed to help him feel better. When his spirits were at their lowest, he would gaze upon them in quiet melancholy till sleep finally came. Their designs seemed to offer the only peace his tired, heartbroken eyes could find.

My tapestries. I had worked on them now for twelve winters, pouring as much hope as I could muster into panel after intricate panel. The only singing I did now, it seemed, was when instilling spells of victory over adversity into the threads. The vibrant reds, yellows, and browns were harder to come by these days, and the feasts and triumphs depicted there existed only in memory. But I had to believe such a time would come again.

There was one panel I longed to create but had not yet begun.

I did not know what form the monster's defeat would take. I prayed daily that wyrd would show me the way.

Chapter Thirteen

I awoke in the night with a gasp. I had dreamt a horrifying dream.

I was underwater, deep in the murky depths of the mere of madness, and in my arms lay little Hrothmund—not a boy as he was now, but a soft, sleeping babe. His blond hair floated about his face, and he wriggled as sleeping babes do.

But as he stretched and yawned, my boy's limbs began to grow, misshapen and grossly transfigured, into tentacles that stretched out toward me. I watched in terror as his sweet face twisted into that of a fiend. Suddenly, he opened his eyes, and they were not little Hrothmund's blue-gray orbs, they were the red-black eyes of the monster.

"I tried to scream," I told Hrothgar as he kindled the lamp at our bedside and leaned over me with concern. "But water filled my mouth, and I could not breathe. I thought that if only I could get us to the surface, the spell would be broken, and Hrothmund would be all right. But I couldn't move. And the babe kept writhing and writhing in my arms—a monster!" I sobbed into his chest.

"Wealtheow," Hrothgar said soothingly, "it was only a dream."

He smoothed my hair in his reassuring way. Nevertheless I sat upright, alarmed by a sudden thought.

"What if it wasn't just a dream? What if it's an omen, a warning of what's to come? Oh Hrothgar, what if our children are next? We must get away from here, away from this endless terror."

The king regarded me silently, then said, "Perhaps your dream does contain a message. We must think on it. But there is no reason to believe our children are in danger. Despite the monster's continued tyranny, the kingdom of the Danes survives. The excursions continue to be successful, and our stores are filled with the spoils of battle."

"Spoils!" I exclaimed. "Of what use to us are treasures when we have no peace of mind? We scrape to get by, producing what the warriors require for the summertime excursions, and little more. We rebuild Heorot and our hopes every summer, only to have them destroyed when the monster makes the great hall its winter's night home."

Hrothgar regarded me calmly. "This is our home," he said simply. "I am Heorot's king, and you are its queen. Its wyrd is our wyrd. We do not leave."

My hysteria faded slowly as I looked into his steady eye.

"Of course," I said. "You are right."

Contemplating the lines in my face, Hrothgar said, "You have not been sleeping. Perhaps Eir can give you something tomorrow to calm your nerves."

"No potion will bring peace," I replied stubbornly. Relenting at his patient gaze, I said, "But I will visit her tomorrow, as you suggest." He smiled, then turned over to extinguish the lamp.

As I lay sleepless in the dark, thinking on the nightmare, I suddenly recalled another dream from long ago. I had been in the forest, and had come upon a nest of birds. Then a wolf howled, and I began to flap my wings as though I were a bird, too.

"You will see a threat, and you will confront it," Mother had said. Her words came back to me as clear as spring water. "A mother—and a queen—must have courage and determination in the face of danger."

"Mother," I whispered, "what am I to do?" From far away, I heard a wolf howl its needless warning. The danger was apparent. I had babes to protect. But how was I to do it? The strength and wisdom of our greatest warriors and advisors had not been able to rid us of the monster. Our women's most well-crafted spells had accomplished nothing. What could I do that had not already been done?

The next morning, I hurried to Eir's quarters, anxious to speak with her about my dream. I found Esher instead, standing outside the door to their home.

"Eir and our daughters are in the forest," he said as I approached. Noting my expression, he asked, "Is there something that troubles you, my queen?"

I hesitated, and said slowly, "I fear for my children, lord advisor. I don't know what I should do to protect them."

He nodded and gazed at me thoughtfully. "You fear the monster," he said. I told him of my dream.

Esher pondered for a moment. "The gods and goddesses provide for each of us in our own way," he said finally. "Though we all come from the same source of life, we each have our own skills and abilities. If you would seek to find the way, let your own wyrd guide you through the great wheel's turning."

As I thought on this, a scout rode up to us in haste. "My lord," he said breathlessly.

"Speak," Esher said.

"A contingent of Heathobards approaches by sea."

"How many?" Esher asked.

"One ship has reached shore, and another is still on the water. It appears that King Ingeld travels with them."

Esher looked at me. "Tell the king," he said to the scout. "I will fetch Unferth and we will meet in the hall." To me, he said, "The princess should be prepared."

"I will see to it," I replied and made quickly for the queen's quarters.

So Ingeld had finally come to Heorot. I had done well in recent years to avoid thinking on it, but it appeared the future could no longer be delayed.

The Danes and Heathobards had verged on conflict for years, ever since Ingeld's father had been killed in battle by Danish troops. Skirmish after skirmish had subsequently made clear that only prolonged conflict would determine a victor. Hrothgar knew our people could not endure both an extended war and the perpetual torment of the monster.

The alternative was to offer Frea to Ingeld as a bride. Like me, and like my mother before me, my daughter was to be a pledge of peace, the knot tying nations together.

I found her in our quarters working a delicate tablet braid. "Frea," I said. Something in my tone alerted her, and she looked up at once, setting the weaving down in her lap.

"Yes, Mother?" she said attentively. I sat down beside her and fingered the well-wrought threads of her design.

"Ingeld king of the Heathobards arrives with a contingent," I said. "You must dress and prepare to pass around the cup."

She nodded. We sat silently for a moment, then I rose to examine her collection of jewelry. Finally I called her attendants. "I return in an hour," I told them. "Dress the princess in her finest and adorn her with the pieces I have selected." They bowed and moved quickly to obey.

"I'll be back," I said to my daughter, who sat motionless on the bed.

"Yes, Mother," she replied, standing up obediently. "I will be ready."

An hour later, we made our way to the great hall where Ingeld and his retinue had just arrived. We stood in the antechamber by the curtained door, listening to Hrothgar's formal greeting.

"Ingeld of the Heathobards," he said, "I welcome you to Heorot. It is an honor to have such worthy warriors in our hall. I pray that you will stay and feast with us today."

"We thank you for this warm welcome," Ingeld replied. "Our business will be brief, but we delight in the Danes' famed hospitality."

And then it was our turn. A guard raised the curtain, and I nudged Frea forward. We entered the room, walking slowly toward the dais. Approaching the throne, I offered the silver horn cup to Hrothgar and uttered the traditional words of blessing. He drank, and returned the cup to me with a reassuring glance.

I turned and gave the cup then to Frea, who took it with both hands. She made her way to the seat of honor where Ingeld sat, and held the mead out to him.

"I bid you take this cup of peace, my lord," she said, "and drink of the blessed mead, that the Heathobards might know the friendship of the Danes."

Ingeld took the cup with a smile, and I saw Frea's cheeks flush a slight crimson. She moved to the advisors' bench and offered the cup in turn to Esher, Unferth, and Hrothulf.

At last my daughter took her place to my left, as I smiled at her encouragingly. She had performed the ceremony perfectly, every bit a gracious hostess. This was the power of women in times of adversity—the ability to offer welcome and comfort, to make a good home, and to provide words of peace and serenity to the people.

She returned my smile tremulously, no doubt relieved that the most difficult part of the ceremony was over.

"I bring gifts of friendship to the Danes," Ingeld said, rising from his seat. He presented Hrothgar with a golden dagger, and Hrothgar gave him an ancestral axe wrought with silver spirals. To Frea, Ingeld presented an armring—the traditional gift of promise.

So my good Frea, raised in such hardship, was now to be sent away to weave peace between nations. It was not easy, but it was the way of things. I took some comfort in knowing that we would have nearly a year to prepare for her departure, as weddings traditionally took place in the fall.

When the repast had begun, Ingeld addressed Hrothgar with cautious respect. "I hear that your people's affliction by the monster of the deep continues," he said.

"That is so," Hrothgar replied. I could hear the weariness in his voice.

"As a tribute to our houses' future joining," Ingeld said, "the Heathobards would seek to end your oppression."

Alarmed, I cast a worried glance at Hrothgar. His expression remained calm, and he spoke quietly.

"Your courage and generosity honor me," he replied. "But many have tried to end our oppression, and all who have done so have died. I no longer seek aid for our suffering. I grew tired of sending warriors to their deaths with no hope for victory or recompense."

"The Heathobard clan is fearsome and strong," Ingeld said proudly. "My warriors have yet to meet an enemy they cannot defeat."

So Frea's husband-to-be would die before they could be married. I glanced at my daughter, who stared apprehensively at the Heathobard king.

"My lord," Esher said. Ingeld looked at him. "The king would not have your blood on his hands. You have come here to create a bond, not destroy one."

"Why is the king of the Danes so certain that death would be the outcome?" Ingeld asked boldly, turning to Hrothgar.

Hrothgar sighed. "I have lost more fine warriors than I care to count these twelve years," he said. "You remember Bersi the Brave. There was none like him for fierce fighting. I never saw a man beat him, and yet the monster snapped him like a stick. And surely your father told you stories of Kylfa and his Warriors of the Spear. Every one of them, famed in song and story, died at the monster's hand. And just last year, a wild tribe of Vladislav warriors from the faraway east perished in the same way. They were valiant, bold, and daring, but the monster lives and they are dead."

"Worst of all," Hrothgar continued, his voice rising slightly, "there is no one to pay the blood price. Their deaths go unrequited."

The king of the Danes spoke with finality. "We could recount those murdered till the sun set and the moon rose," he said. "Then the monster would come to us, Ingeld, and it would kill us as it has killed every warrior who has dared oppose it these twelve long years."

The room was silent.

"I see," Ingeld said at last.

When night came, Dane and Heathobard alike retired to the outbuildings.

Winter was coming and the weather had been poor, but the day after Ingeld and his warriors left was warm and clear. In preparation for my morning's undertaking, I told Muni I had business with Eir, and informed Eir that I had business with Muni. My attendants I sent on various time-consuming errands.

When I was alone at last and certain no one was watching, I made my way out of the village and into the forest. I walked for an hour until I reached the end of the woods our people frequented, and entered the older forest surrounding the afflicted lake.

Hrothgar's conversation with Ingeld had made it clear—the way of the warriors was not working. Even our women's magic had failed. Yet I was the one with babes to protect—and as Esher said, I must let my own wyrd guide me.

That wyrd was forever entwined with the ancient mere. Mother had come to me on this lake, and my prayers at its shore helped give me my Freu, I was sure of it. Inhabited by creatures of darkness or no, this was what I knew to do. The thread of my life drew me here, and I felt certain the web of all our lives would be woven by my actions. Esher had said, we each have our own skills and abilities given to us by the gods and goddesses. My love for my children and my faith in this lake were my gifts.

My faith . . . in the mere of madness.

For twelve years no one had dared come to the lake that had given me my child. Not since the monster had turned it into a cursed bog of death and Hrothgar alone returned from its poisonous shore had any human ventured there.

I was terrified. First, I was afraid that after all these years I would not be able to find it, that the path would have disappeared, or my memory of the way would fail me. Second, I was afraid I was about to die.

I made my way through the cold damp of the forest, shivering with chill and fear. As I approached the clearing in the trees, no bird sang there, and no creature scurried on the leaf-littered ground. The branches of the trees were bare and skeletal.

I came out at last on the rocky ledge at the lake's edge, and was shocked by the change in its once-clear waters. Steam rose from the roiling blackness, and foul creatures swam just below the surface of the filthy waves.

Shaking, I got down on my knees beside the poisonous tarn. At any moment the monster might appear and dash me to pieces on the rock, or take my head between its teeth and squeeze out my brains.

My hands trembled as I reached into my underdress and pulled out a scrap of cloth. Measuring only a hand's span, it was all I had time to make for the offering. Into this bit of cloth I had woven all my love for my children and my people, along with a desperate spell of cleansing and renewal.

I put the weaving on the ground in front of me and, quivering, closed my eyes and prayed. I offered prayers of supplication for wholeness to the gods and goddesses. I prayed to the lake, begging for purity and safety. I wove my prayer like a tapestry, fashioned from twelve years of pain and a desperate love.

Still shaking, I finished my spell and opened my eyes. The rank water bubbled, and foul creatures swam, but I was alive. As I gazed at the steaming surface, it flashed for a moment with sunlight, though there were only clouds above. It flashed again, and for a moment the water seemed to clear, then become murky. At the third flash, I understood: For all its blood-blackened waves and noxious mist, the lake was clean. Its ancient pureness may not have been able to repel the creature who had invaded it, but this foulness was a deception. Somewhere deep below the monsters and the filth, the sacred mere's essence remained intact.

I sighed with relief and the beginnings of hope. Resistance seemed suddenly possible. I must return to Heorot and decide what form the endeavor should take.

My thoughts were interrupted by the sound of an animal rustling heavily in the dead, tangled brush. Still on my knees, I froze as a large-snouted creature came out of the wood and slunk down to the water. The size of a wolf but more akin to a rodent, its curved claws and sharp-toothed grin were like nothing I had ever seen.

I watched, terrified, as the creature stared intently into the murky water that lapped between the bank's twisted roots. With a swift, sudden gesture it scooped the water and came up with a small fetid beast in its gnarled claw. The fishlike thing writhed for an instant, then the creature tore it apart, slurping down bones and all.

I knew if I moved, my fate would be the same.

The foul wind that blew over the lake had so far kept it from smelling that I was near. Heart pounding, rocks digging into my knees, I trembled slightly and watched as it peered into the water again. I thought I saw a small ripple on the foul surface, and knew I did when the creature followed the subtle motion with its head. It made a quick swipe and began to pull another small fishlike thing from the water.

But its prey suddenly exploded into the air. I saw with a shock that the small fish was not a fish at all, but part of a larger creature endowed with a lure that dangled from its head. The water beast opened enormous, razor-toothed jaws and snatched up the wolf-rodent. The doomed creature's limbs kicked and clawed the air, and then it was gone. I stared uncomprehending, stunned by this unexpected, life-saving turn, as the monster fish slapped into the depths with a fetid splash.

A sudden wind whipped the black waves of the mere even higher, and the water began to bubble up, gasping with little explosions as though something very deep were coming to the surface. I scrambled off the ledge and ran back into the forest, imagining the monster behind me the whole way. When I could run no further, I stumbled and lurched, looking back over my shoulder with a rising panic. At last I came out of the woods and into the village. I raced to my quarters. Entering the room, I closed the door breathlessly and leaned my cheek against it, panting. Suddenly, there was a noise behind me, and I whirled with a gasp.

Chapter Fourteen

Muni and Eir stood looking at me, their arms crossed and brows furrowed with almost the same expression.

"Where have you been?" Muni asked. "We were so worried."

"I'm fine," I said, still panting. I threw myself down on the bed as they stared at me with concern.

"You don't look fine," Muni said. Eir sat down next to me and put her hand on my head.

"You are flushed and hot," she said.

"That's no surprise," I said. "I have been running for over an hour."

"We were about to alert the king that you were missing," Muni said. "Where were you?"

They stared at me expectantly while I looked at the ground.

"I went to the lake," I said finally.

"The lake," Muni repeated slowly. "What do you mean—the mere?" she gasped. "The mere of madness?"

"Yes," I replied.

"Wealtheow," Eir said seriously. "I cannot understand why you would take such a risk. You could have been killed."

"I know."

"Why? Why did you do this?" Muni asked, incredulous.

Agitated despite my weariness, I stood up and pointed vigorously toward the hall. "The warriors' way has failed—we all know it! How many of our people have died attempting the same futile strategy over and over? I can no longer wait for others—or even wyrd—to save us. I must do it myself."

From the pain in their faces, I could tell my friends understood my profound frustration. We had suffered together for twelve long years. I sighed and sat down beside Eir, taking her hand. I looked up at Muni.

"I don't know how," I said, "but it must be done. I am queen, and I will not see my people tortured any longer."

I told them then of the lake, of its foulness and my prayers. I recounted how the surface of the water had flashed, and shared my perception that its squalor was a deception aimed to protect it. I described the strange incident with the monster fish in that dead place, and how it had killed the wolf-rodent. Finally I explained how the water had begun to bubble as though something from down deep was coming to the surface, and terror had suddenly overtaken me, and I had run and walked and run again all the way back to Heorot.

Muni asked a few questions but Eir remained quiet while I spoke. When I had recounted everything, we sat silently for a while, all of us trying to decipher what it meant.

At last Eir said, "You are very brave, Wealtheow. We have had many false hopes and failed efforts over the years, but somehow what happened at the mere makes me hopeful. It may be that good comes of what you have ventured."

"You could have been killed," Muni objected.

"I had to act," I said weakly. I felt suddenly exhausted, as though I could sleep for a week. I had used all the energy and courage I possessed, and now I was drained of everything but the need to close my eyes.

"We should let her rest," Eir told Muni. They rose to go.

"You must promise us you will not go there again," Muni said.

I looked at her thoughtfully.

"Or at least talk to us if you are considering it," she insisted.

I gave a weary smile. "I promise."

I felt better for having told my friends. It lessened my apprehension to remember that we were in this together. Still, I could not decipher the meaning of all that I had seen—and it seemed important to make it out.

Winter blew through Heorot, and the solstice approached. It was time again for Yule.

We observed the holiday as ever, but much about how we celebrated had changed. We could not have our Yule log, which had once burned day and night, so we relit a bonfire every morning. Activities for each of the seven days had to be concluded by sundown.

And thus in a somewhat saddened, abbreviated way did we mark the longest night of the year. The sun's return was more desired than ever, for with the short winter days came less time spent in camaraderie and more time closed in our separate spaces, fearing the dark. Heorot belonged to the creature at night.

On the final day of Yule, the people assembled in the ring of gathering for the reading. The giant bonfire had been lit under a gray sky. Our children knew nothing of rushing off to feed

Sleipnir, Odin's eight-legged horse. Instead they were herded into the hall to play while the most important, and grimmest, rituals of the solstice were observed. It was not Odin and the Wild Hunt we feared. It was the inexplicable and insatiable wrath of the monster who ruled our nights.

Hrothgar and I sat in the thrones on the stage to one side of the fire as Esher carried the telling stone into the ring of gathering. Its deeply carved surface spoke of mysteries—spirals, discs, and runes revealing the wyrd of the Danes. Yet since the monster had come, the message had been ever the same: much suffering in store for the people. It was a telling we would rather not hear, but one we were nevertheless compelled to seek out.

Esher made his way slowly through the crowd to the stage and placed the stone on the podium. "Yesterday, today, and tomorrow," he intoned. "So the people were, so they are, and so they shall be, till the twilight of the gods."

He stepped back and Hrothgar stood, raising his arms into the air. "The Lady Eir will divine," the king announced.

Eir stepped forward. I looked at her fondly in her mothering dress, forgetting my worry for a moment. She was expecting her fourth child in early summer. "Esher is so happy," she had told me. "He cherishes our daughters, but he hopes for a son."

Eir placed her hands slowly on the telling stone. "At the height of darkness, we gather to see the way," she said, tracing the shapes and letters with her fingertips.

I found myself hoping that the future would be different this time, as I did every year.

The drums throbbed their hypnotic beat and people crowded thickly about the stage while Eir gazed silently into the fire. At last she turned to the king, a curious expression on her face. I leaned forward alertly. What had she seen?

"As the winter wind sweeps in to blow away the leaves of autumn, so too comes a conqueror to Heorot." She paused for a moment, her tired face suddenly awakened with hope. "A conqueror not of men, but of darkness. This is what I see."

Her words rippled through the multitude. Yule after Yule, the stone had brought only news of continued suffering—but now this. The people began to sing, a few at first, then more, until all of Heorot chanted a song of rekindling.

Then they danced, one person following the next in a circle that spiraled ever in upon itself. When the dance was finished, people began to chatter excitedly, moving away from the ring of gathering and toward their sleeping quarters. Despite this good news, there would be no lingering celebration, and everyone would be indoors before nightfall.

And so the longest night of the year passed, and the daylight ascended.

I woke the next morning to see Hrothgar gazing down on me impatiently. "I bid you good morning, my queen," he said with feigned formality.

I laughed. "And to you a good morning, my lord," I replied. "I hope I have not inconvenienced you by slumbering when you would have me awake."

"It was growing tiresome," he agreed, "but all is well." Clearing his throat, he said, "I have been thinking about the reading."

"Your heart is hopeful," I replied, examining his face.

"Yes." Glancing around the room, he added, "I have also been thinking about your tapestries."

"My tapestries?"

He nodded and looked down at me. "I believe it is time you began work on the final panel."

Tears rose in my eyes. "My lord," I said. "I begin today."

Chapter Fifteen

The Danes had been given hope that a hero was coming to deliver us from our oppression. But we didn't know when. Today? Tomorrow? Next season? Next year? As the initial excitement over Eir's Yuletide divination faded, life continued much as it had since the monster's occupation. We were a people used to waiting.

"It might not even be a person," Muni had pointed out wryly. "It could be a plague or illness that kills the monster."

Spring came, and I began to spend more time outdoors, though I did not venture near the lake. Frea and I took frequent walks as we discussed the many details of her upcoming wedding and marriage. She knew much about being a queen, but I still had more to teach her.

One sunny afternoon, we took advantage of the dry weather and ventured out to the rolling dunes that collared the coast. My daughter was memorizing her wedding lines well, but I could tell the pull of the sea was strong, so after a while I let her go down to the shore. As I meandered alone through the sandy hills, I saw that all here was reborn. Springtime surged with little yellow sandflowers and bright green seagrasses, and tiny birds twittered a song of awakening.

I did not sense the season's rebirth in myself. Despite the world's renewal, all I felt was tired and old, worn out deep down where the bird's song and the flower's delicate beauty could not reach. It seemed another lifetime when I had been Frea's age, planning for my new life in the kingdom of the Danes. That eagerly antici-pated adventure had not turned out as I had imagined. Whatever was left of this life had best come soon, because I had little energy left for it.

Frea ran toward me then over the dunes, shimmering with excitement.

"A steed on the waves!" she exclaimed.

I hurried after her toward the sea. From a safe distance—but still near enough to observe—we peered over the top of one of the sandy dunes. The surf roared against the beach, drowning out all other sound.

I saw the curved prow of a foreign ship pulled up onto the sand. As a contingent of warriors began to disembark from the handsome vessel, the booming surf seemed to become music for the tale their shining armor told.

Adorned in full battle gear—lustrous iron-ringed mail shirts polished like silver, sturdy helmets glittering with gold—the war-riors strode purposefully onto the beach. Their spears and swords shone in the sun, a mighty militia of light.

We watched with fascination as the strangers were greeted by the mounted Danish patrol. I could distinguish their leader even before he stepped forward to speak to the guard. As his retinue fell in behind him, Frea drew in her breath and let it out with an extended "Ohhh." I gave her a sharp look, though secretly I shared the sentiment.

I had never seen a larger warrior. His massive, unyielding torso seemed hardly to need the protection of armor. Great muscles tightened as he raised his arm to salute the guard. I could not make out the features beneath the faceplate of his crested helmet, but somehow I knew they were pleasing.

I tore my eyes finally from the lead warrior and gazed upon all the troops. Though none approached the majesty of their leader, they were a fine, fresh group of fighters. Any one of them looked a match for our best. The contingent was small, so I knew they had not come for warfare. A mission of diplomacy, perhaps? That would be a waste of muscle. My heart sank as another thought occurred. Perhaps they had come to fight the monster.

After conferring with the guard, the leader beckoned to his troops, and the unfamiliar warriors began making their way toward Heorot. Frea and I waited for a moment, listening to the clanking of their armor as it rang out across the dunes. The sound seemed to awaken something that had been sleeping in the world. Suddenly breeze-blown, the sand sparkled, the seagrass gleamed, and the yellow flowers fluttered.

"Come," I told Frea. When we reached the village, I sent her to fetch Muni. "And then get dressed," I added. "Your best dress and finest jewelry." As she hurried off to comply, I proceeded calmly to the hall, heart pounding.

Entering the antechamber, I heard the mysterious warrior begin to greet my husband the king. I moved quickly to the curtained door between the rooms.

"I salute you, Hrothgar," he said. "I am Beowulf, son of Ecgtheow, a loyal kinsman of King Hygelac of the Geats. As a young warrior I have been the victor in many great struggles.

"It came recently to my ears that a monster held the Danes captive in their own hall. Visiting sailors spoke of how it ruled distinguished Heorot by night. I determined then to sail across the sea in search of this creature. My elders encouraged me, for they know of my strength. They have seen me dripping with the blood of my enemies in battle, and they were there when I destroyed giants who threatened our people. I have dispatched in the dead of night numerous creatures of the deep, and I seek to conquer this one."

I had never heard such a bold speech.

"I come to kill your monster for you," the warrior continued, "though I ask that you let us Geats do it alone. If the gods and goddesses have decided it is my time to die—if the monster is successful in dragging the best of us to its filthy lair, spraying our blood across the water—then the Danes will have no need of funeral rites for me. I ask only that you send my armor back to Hygelac. It is a well-crafted heirloom that belonged to my grandfather. I do not concern myself with the outcome, for wyrd will ever go its way."

I leaned against the curtain to hear how my husband would respond to the young warrior's daring words.

"Good Beowulf," Hrothgar said warmly, "You come to us in friendship, and we are grateful. I remember when your father was in need of protection long ago. For fear of war, his own people could not shelter him from his pursuers. So Ecgtheow sailed to the Danes for help. I was a young king then; my older brother, a better man than I, had just died. But I settled the feud with treasure and your father acknowledged our bond.

"It pains me to tell you of the misery our people have suffered," Hrothgar said with a sigh. "Of the grief the monster has brought us. My warriors have dwindled and the Danes are weary. Fate has not been kind to us."

He nodded at the massive warrior. "I have heard tell of your adventures across the sea. It is said you have the strength of thirty men in just one hand's grip. And it is plain you have courage. But I must tell you, Lord Beowulf, many brave men have vowed to end our suffering, and all of them died at the monster's hand."

Hrothgar's voice was kindly as he said, "Let us enjoy our fellowship here today. The Danes prepare a banquet in your honor. We will speak of past victories, and ponder future triumph."

Then the mead flowed, and the Geats and Danes began to talk with one another. Excitement animated our people. The visiting warriors' dynamic presence stood in stark contrast to our weary existence.

Muni entered the antechamber and came up to me at the curtained door.

"What is it?" she whispered.

"Warriors from across the sea," I whispered back. She put her eye to a small gap between the curtain and the doorframe.

"My goodness," she said breathlessly. "Look at them."

"I know," I agreed. "We must get dressed."

In the queen's quarters, I searched through my clothes chest till I found what I was seeking. Removing the blue dress from beneath the other items, I shook it in the air with a snap. The fabric rippled like the sea, and I felt suddenly giddy. I had not worn my treasured wedding dress for years, but somehow it seemed perfect for the occasion. Muni raised an eyebrow but said nothing. She went quickly through my jewelry, choosing the pieces she knew I would prefer to wear.

"Who are they?" she asked, securing the silver brooches at my shoulders.

"Geats," I said. "Their leader is Beowulf, son of Ecgtheow, a noble warrior who came to Hrothgar for help long ago."

"Do you think the king will allow him to remain in the hall at nightfall?"

"I don't know," I mused, sliding a large ring of twisted gold onto my upper arm. "It is possible."

Muni finished fastening my shoes and stood up. "There," she said. "You look beautiful."

"Beauty is for the young," I replied. "It will suffice to be the queen." She laughed and we made our way quickly back to the hall, my jewelry jingling as I walked.

The servants bustled about in preparation for the repast. As Muni directed their efforts, I listened to the warriors' conversation in the main room. With growing unease, I realized that Lord Unferth had indulged quite heavily in the cup since the Geats' arrival. I could hear the mead in his voice as he spoke to their leader.

"Here now," he said loudly. "Are you the same Beowulf who foolishly challenged Breca to a swimming contest?"

The room fell silent, and Unferth continued, "Yes, I recall it now. Your elders tried to dissuade you, but the two of you were headstrong and would not hear reason. For a week you battled the waves, tossed about by the furious sea. On the seventh day, I have heard it told, Breca found his way to shore before you. He made good his claim and was proved the stronger man."

The contempt in Unferth's voice alarmed me. He should know that such rudeness was contrary to our laws of hospitality. Welcomed guests were never greeted with harsh words. I wondered what Hrothgar would do.

Unferth finished his story, stumbling a bit over the words as they fell out of his mouth. "That noble warrior went on to rule the Brisings—the Brondings," he said, "a wise king loved by all. As for you, Lord Beowulf, you may have done well in battle, but it will take more than boasts to handle the monster that terrorizes Heorot."

There was a short silence, and then the Geat leader's voice rang throughout the hall. "My Lord Unferth," he said. "You would speak knowledgeably on matters widely rumored but little known. I would be delighted to provide you with the sobering truth."

I grinned at his composure as Muni came to stand beside me at the curtain. We listened eagerly to the Geat warrior's tale.

"Breca and I, it is true, grew up together," he said, "childhood friends who took pleasure in games and contests of strength. We had long spoken of a swimming competition, and one year, when we had grown sufficiently strong of limb, the opportunity presented itself.

"We swam together in the sea for five long days. Breca could not lose me and I would not leave him, but finally a storm drove us apart. The fury of the tempest must have awakened the depths. A monster soon appeared, fierce and foul.

"It dragged me to the bottom of the ocean, and if not for the iron rings of my armor, I would have perished in its terrible jaws. The battle raged on, and I managed finally to give the creature a fatal taste of my sword. Then other monsters swarmed me, trying to devour what the first had not. Hoping to feast on my flesh, they tasted instead the same well-wrought iron the other had savored. All counted, I killed nine deadly beasts of the sea."

As the Geat warrior described his battle with the water monsters, I envisioned the bubbling mere and the writhing creatures I had seen there. None compared to their master, the cruel monster Beowulf now proposed to defeat.

He continued, "I landed then on the shore of Finland and made my way back to my home. I have not heard such a tale told of you, Lord Unferth, nor of Breca, but this account of my own exploits is a tale of fact not fancy.

"The tales of Lord Unferth," Beowulf frowned, "rumor the killing of kin, but it is not to me that he will answer for that."

I checked a gasp. The Geat leader had uttered aloud that which, in all my time with the Danes, had only been whispered. And yet Hrothgar still allowed him to speak.

"The monster who terrorizes your people," Beowulf said, staring at Unferth, "could never have done so were you as brave and valiant as you think you are. This hateful creature will soon discover it cannot so easily defeat the Geats. When the sun rises tomorrow, any who desire will be able to enter this hall without fear. The despised intruder will lie vanquished."

The room was hushed, and then the king spoke. "I am pleased, Lord Beowulf," Hrothgar said. "Your courage is undeniable, and I see that your spirit is resolute."

Pressed against the other side of the curtained door, I knew at once what he would say. "I welcome you and your warriors to spend the night in our hall."

So the Geats would be allowed to battle the monster. Muni and I exchanged concerned glances. I was elated by the possibility that Beowulf might be the conqueror spoken of in the runes, but also frightened at the thought of these mighty warriors being killed in our hall.

"I must tend to the guard, my lord," Unferth said, rising abruptly. The people began to talk again cheerfully, the long-forgotten sounds of happy conversation rising up to the rafters.

After a moment the curtained door was swept aside and Unferth pushed past me, muttering under his breath. "That arrogant Geat thinks he can kill the monster in his sleep," he said bitterly. "We'll see how brave he is when the floorboards run slick with his blood."

As the angry words sank in, I felt a sudden thrill of recognition. That was it. I knew what must be done.

Chapter Sixteen

I smoothed my hair with my hands and arranged the golden circlet on my head. As she handed me the jeweled horn cup, Muni whispered, "Don't be nervous." I rolled my eyes at her and she smirked. After all these years, my childhood friend had never grown tired of teasing me.

"I am ready," I said, and the guard drew aside the curtained door.

The warriors fell respectfully silent as I entered the great hall. Though my eyes were on Hrothgar, I was acutely aware of the Geat contingent who sat watching the procession.

I approached the throne and held the cup out with a smile. "My lord," I addressed the king warmly. "I offer you this flowing cup, and beg of you to drink. It is said a wise ruler knows when to speak and when to listen. May the king of the Danes, who is so dear to his people, be wise in his dealings and generous with his gold. I invite you to take pleasure in the repast we have prepared."

Hrothgar drank and returned the horn cup to me. "Let us all enjoy one another's company today," he replied.

I passed the cup then to Esher and Unferth, who sat as ever on the advisors' bench to the king's right. Unferth seemed to have recovered his composure, and took the cup from me with his usual lack of expression. Esher smiled and thanked me as always. Next I proceeded to Hrothulf and my sons, who sat to the left of our thrones.

Finally I carried the cup to Beowulf. The Geat leader had been given the place of honor, a raised bench directly across from the king. Muni had been right—I was strangely nervous. Holding the horn cup out with both hands, I raised my eyes to his.

"We welcome you, Lord Beowulf," I said. "Drink, and know the hospitality of the Danes."

He was young and handsome, with shoulder-length hair perfectly framing a strong, determined face. His expression as we looked at each other was open and inquiring, and I felt certain he was going to ask me a question. Instead he completed the ritual in the traditional way, taking the horn cup from my hands with a respectful nod and drinking deep. He wiped his mouth with satisfaction and returned the cup to me.

A sudden happiness sprang up in me at the sight of these powerful warriors. They had undertaken an arduous journey across the sea with the single goal of delivering us from our suffering. "I thank the gods and goddesses," I said, "for answering our prayers and bringing a hero to end our affliction."

At my words, the Geat leader's jaw set and a light of excitement came to his eyes. I saw then in his countenance the love of danger and eagerness for action that must so terrify his foes.

Beowulf leaned forward intently. "My lady," he replied. "When I resolved to rid your people of this creature, in my heart I knew the struggle would conclude in either victory or death." Holding out his hands and turning his palms up, he said, "I offer you these hands, and a promise—I will kill your monster for you, or die trying."

I felt the warmth of the Geat warrior's resolve. My uncertainty burned away in the heat of its determined blaze. Smiling, I handed the horn cup to a servant and returned to the throne, taking my place at Hrothgar's side.

The king stood and raised his arm into the air. "Let the feast begin," he announced.

The musicians struck up at once, and their songs seemed the sweetest I had heard in a long time. Hope rippled through the crowd like wind over the sea. We reveled in the unexpected celebration as warrior after warrior toasted to the Geats' success and the destruction of the monster. I could not remember tasting a better repast than the peppered fish the servants put before us. As though for the first time I noticed the flickering firelight that danced on the warriors' armor and glinted in the ladies' jewelry. Heorot seemed almost to have recaptured some of its long-forgotten glory.

As the people chatted cheerfully, I observed Beowulf working his way around the room, conversing with his warriors or stopping to talk with an inquisitive Dane. Every nearby woman watched from the corner of her eye, while every warrior vied subtly for the Geat leader's attention. To each he was gracious, his actions proper and courteous. I found myself wishing my boys had such manners.

As Hrothgar and Esher discussed the upcoming summer excursions, Beowulf came to me and knelt at my throne. I waved him up, impressed with the pious formality.

"I trust you are enjoying our hospitality, Lord Beowulf?" I said.

"Yes, my lady," he replied. "A warm meal does much to slough off the salt of travel."

He gazed at me curiously. It was not an impolite stare, but

rather a look of recognition, though it was certain we had never laid eyes on one another before. I returned his gaze with a benign smile, trying to find the appropriate words to move us beyond this strange silence. It had been many years since I had experienced one of those conversational circumstances Mother was ever coaching me on as a girl.

"I heard the words you exchanged with Lord Unferth," I said, and immediately chided myself. Would I never learn to think before speaking?

A hint of a smile came to the warrior's face. "Yes," he replied. "One must always speak the truth. Thor knows, the reputation a warrior earns in life is all that will endure. I trust Lord Unferth harbors no ill will."

"Certainly not," I replied, though I wasn't so sure.

He looked at me candidly. "The Queen of the Danes prayed a hero would come."

"Yes." I had determined to stay with short, safe answers.

"You cast spells to put an end to your suffering." In his statement I heard the same unspoken question that had lingered earlier.

"Our women have cast many spells, to no avail," I replied cautiously. It was obvious the Geat warrior was trying to get at something. But I was not certain I was ready to reveal it.

"You speak your way to truth, my lady," he said frankly. "I heard it when you offered me the cup."

I looked at him carefully.

"There is a lake," I said finally. "A place of ancient healing and fertility for the Danes. It gave my babes life."

He nodded, and I told him briefly of my journey to the mere.

"A courageous act," he said. Glancing at Hrothgar, who

remained engrossed in debate with the advisors, he asked, "Does your husband the king know of your visit?"

"No," I replied simply.

He nodded and looked down for a moment. "Why do you speak of it?"

"Because you need to know," I said. "I believe the monster has a weakness."

His eyes narrowed. "I am listening."

"My husband is a good king, beloved by his people," I said. "But he is getting older. The responsibilities of an elderly king differ greatly from those of a young warrior. He must worry not just for himself or his kin or his glory, but for a nation. He cannot cast his own safety aside for heroics. He must be wise and fair. It is a burden King Hrothgar has carried as well as anyone could through these long, difficult years."

Beowulf nodded, wondering, no doubt, where my words were leading.

"But for you," I told him, "a young warrior of great strength and nerve, life is more straightforward. You fight, and you win. After twelve years of watching brave warriors perish, however, I am certain it will take something more to prevail."

Beowulf listened intently.

"When the monster comes," I said. "You must not seem all that you are. You must be the predator that appears to be prey."

"To seem less than I am," he replied, thinking quickly. "Hide somehow?"

"Not hide," I said. "Slumber."

He merely looked at me.

"When the monster comes," I explained, "it will expect armed warriors ready for combat, or no warriors at all. What it will not anticipate are warriors who sleep as though they have retired to the safety of a shrine. And in this feigned sleep, should you, Lord Beowulf, post yourself near the door, the creature's surprise would be your opportunity."

He nodded thoughtfully. "I have heard it said that no weapon can harm the monster."

"None has," I agreed.

"So it will be hand to hand," he mused.

"A hand the monster will not expect," I replied.

"Just so," he said. "Thank you for your insight."

I smiled at his acceptance. The Geat leader peered at me, wrapped in his thoughts.

"My queen is something like you," he said almost wistfully. "Queen Hygd, Hygelac's wife. She moves the people to greatness with her energy and inspiration."

I saw in the warrior a bit of the boy he must have been not so long ago. A young man possessed of great power and idealism, he might someday make an excellent king. If he survived the night.

"I thank you for those kind words," I said. "The gods and goddesses have given us each our own special gift, and it is up to us to do with it what we can." I smiled to myself at this mixture of my mother's and Esher's wisdom.

We remained in thoughtful silence as the repast came to its close. His business with the advisors concluded, Hrothgar stood and raised his arm into the air. The multitude rose with him.

"My people," the king of the Danes pronounced solemnly. "The sun is setting, and evening comes."

Approaching Beowulf, he embraced him and said, "In all the years I have ruled Heorot, this is the first time I leave it entirely in another's keeping. Care well for this meadhall, Lord Beowulf, and keep your mind on the enemy. I pray that wyrd may guide you, and the gods and goddesses be with you. Splendid treasure will be yours if you see this dark night through."

Turning, the king extended his hand to me and we proceeded from the great hall. The Danish warriors and their ladies filed after us, suddenly somber. At the door, I looked back at the Geat contingent, valiant and ready for action in their gleaming battle gear.

Beowulf's face in the firelight was keen and unyielding. I knew soon he would put down his weapons, remove his armor, and lie in silent wait for the monster. I wondered whether I would see him again—or if morning would find his lifeblood splattered on the walls, like that of so many heroes before him.

Chapter Seventeen

In my quarters, Hrothgar leaned over to examine the tapestry I had recently completed. I did not know whether the scene it depicted was prophecy or merely optimism. The picture had come to me one night soon after Yule, when I woke suddenly in the darkness, as I did more often these days. I could not recall who had been speaking in my dream, but the image remained clear in my mind, and I wove it into the final panel of the tapestry.

The great hall stood proudly, its intricately threaded outline shining golden in the sunlight. Beside it, a warrior held up the head of the monster. Stitched droplets of blood, tiny and red, fell from the contorted visage to the ground, and where they fell little white flowers blossomed forth.

"Let us hope this comes to pass," Hrothgar said, moving to sit beside me on the bed. "Perhaps tonight is the night."

I looked into his worn face and smiled gently at my husband. "Perhaps tomorrow we will hang these tapestries in triumph on the walls of the great hall," I said. "Before today, I had almost forgotten what it is to have hope. But now I am fairly filled with it. Oh, Hrothgar, do you think he is the one?"

"I do not know," he replied quietly. "In all my years of battle, I have never seen another like him. His strength is apparent, and his very presence speaks to vast courage. What's more, he is steadfast in his purpose. His will is immense.

"Nevertheless," he continued slowly, "many great warriors have died in this effort. Some of them had never lost in combat until the monster struck them down and crunched their bones in its teeth. Only wyrd will reveal whether Beowulf is to be the deliverer of Heorot, or merely the creature's next prey."

"I believe in him," I said.

The king looked at me shrewdly for a moment. "As do I," he replied, and then, "Your conversation during the repast appeared quite serious."

"We spoke of the monster," I said.

Later, as Hrothgar slept fitfully beside me, I lay awake imagining what Beowulf and his warriors must be feeling as they waited in the great hall.

Perhaps they believed they would never see their loved ones again. As they put aside their weapons and stretched out to rest, their closest companion was now the ghostly memory of those who had come before—scores of ill-fated warriors who had likewise waited for the creature.

Perhaps the Geat warriors envisioned their homeland with nostalgia, thinking on their families, their childhood stomping grounds—everything they must tell good-bye. If wyrd willed it, they would breathe their last tonight in the great hall. But this was a venture they had vowed to pursue. For the promise of gold and glory, these warriors intended to rid the Danes of their suffering, or die.

Faraway, I heard a howl that chilled my heart. The darkness was coming.

As the other Geats slumbered, Beowulf lay sleepless, watching and waiting near the door. Night fell, then deepened into blackness.

Without warning, the monster burst into the hall, ripping the iron-barred doors off their hinges in an instant, leaving a great hole where seconds before an impermeable entrance had stood.

Iron-clad doors had never been able to keep Grendel out, nor had the countless spells cast by the women. The usual protections had failed the people time and time again. Victory ever belonged to the terrible invader, who by now believed himself invincible, a god. Certainly he had no reason to suppose that his tyranny could ever be challenged.

Mighty Heorot, the greatest hall ever built, had been constructed as a monument to the supremacy of the Danes. Yet for these past twelve years it had been ruled not by a king, but by a monster. For all its misfortune, the building itself remained the largest, strongest meadhall in the world. None less than Grendel could have shorn its timbers.

As he approached Heorot that night, the marauder expected no men, or at the very least no fight. He had never known a contest. The presence of humans was an unanticipated delight—a gift of flesh for no special occasion.

Only Beowulf heard the unnerving laughter, the creature's vile delight at the prospect of engorging these slumbering warriors. Resisting the impulse to act, the Geat leader lay still as the monster crept toward him.

Grendel approached, intrigued by the prone figures. He sniffed the air, then bent over the nearest body and stared into its face. His mouth watered. He flexed his knotted fingers and reached to crush the skull of his prey.

He felt the pressure and cracking of fragile bones. A sudden, vicious, pain tore through him.

Grendel was astonished to find himself in a deathgrip. His muscles tensed and he froze in a shock of revelation as fiendish claw encountered determined handclasp.

Eyes met in the flickering firelight. Monster and hero glared in an instant of recognition that could not have been less anticipated by one, or more desired by the other. Grendel experienced then what had been widely familiar to his victims: terror.

Startled, he attempted to disengage from the warrior's fearsome grip, twisting his body with a jerk and wringing his claws in an effort to break free. No longer desiring his dinner, he sought only the safety of his lair.

But there would be no fast getaway. Beowulf had gripped the monster like a vise. As the words of his vow came back to inspire him, the Geat leader leapt up and tightened his grasp on the horrible claw.

Grendel shrieked with a petrifying sound that shook the rafters of the great hall. Terrified into wakefulness, the rest of the Geat warriors leapt to their feet and snatched up their weapons in a panic. They circled quickly around the battling pair, but could only watch as their leader closed with the monster, slamming into benches and ricocheting off walls as Grendel struggled to break the lethal grip.

No onslaught by the creature had ever approached the devastation this battle now inflicted on the great hall. The clash between Beowulf and Grendel was by far the harshest injury it had ever endured. No Dane would have believed it could be so ravaged.

Around the hall they banged and flew, the monster trying ever to yank his claw from the warrior's mighty grip. As the two combatants paused for breath, panting, Beowulf spoke for the first time.

"Your life means nothing," he said softly from between clenched teeth.

Grendel howled again, tortured and desperate in the grasp of the strongest man alive. With a sudden sundering sound, the massive shoulder snapped, bones shattering in a brutal wellspring of blood. Beowulf gave a wrenching jerk, and the monstrous arm came off in his hand.

For an instant, everything stopped. Grendel fell silent, staring dumbly at the warrior before him. Beowulf stood motionless, the dripping limb quivering in his powerful grasp.

The pain came like a blast of fire blazing through the misshapen body. With a hideous moan, Grendel turned and ran for the hole where the door had been. Grasping the torn socket, he staggered away, leaving a trail of flowing gore.

The Geat warriors shouted in fierce joy as Beowulf shook the severed limb triumphantly in the air. A mortal wound, Heorot was purged at last.

Chapter Eighteen

As word of the great battle spread, warriors from all over the Danish kingdom assembled to examine the monster's tracks. They set out to follow the bloody trail, leading a mounted expedition to discover where the doomed creature had gone. They hoped to come across its lifeless body somewhere in the woods, but instead eventually found themselves at the shores of the afflicted lake.

None of the company had ever seen a body of water so foul. The surface roiled with filth and steamed with blood. But the monster was nowhere to be seen.

Cautiously, a handful of warriors dismounted to see what had become of the trail. They ascertained that the bloody tracks disappeared at the shore.

"It has made its way back to its lair to die," said one seasoned chieftain. The warriors shouted with joy. Leaping onto their shining horses, they rode quickly back to Heorot, eager to report the happy news.

It was a cheerful ride. Over and over they retold the story, already legend, of how Beowulf had wrenched the monster's arm from its body and dealt the fatal blow. "There is none like him for strength and boldness," they repeated to one another. "No greater warrior anywhere on earth."

A talented old warrior spun a song of Beowulf's conquest, and entertained them with tales of other gallant heroes. On a straight section of the path back to the great hall, they let their battle steeds take the lead.

Sensing their masters' joy, the high-spirited horses galloped with all their might, hooves pounding into the earth. Their streaming manes of red, yellow, and black gleamed in the mid-morning sun. Warriors and mounts alike rejoiced to be alive on this magnificent day.

At last the contingent came thundering up to Heorot, eager to see the final evidence of Beowulf's triumph. From protruding shoulder bone to hideous curved claw, the creature's defeat was apparent in the grisly trophy that hung in the rafters of the great hall. Beowulf's supremacy was clear. The warriors loitered, talking and laughing and gazing at the limb in amazement.

In my quarters, a servant announced Esher and he entered the chamber where the royal retinue waited. All morning we had heard the tales, though they seemed so wonderful I had trouble believing them. We had listened for any small bit of news. While I dressed, Muni ran to find her husband Wulfgat, who was among those tracking the fatally wounded creature. She returned, breathless, and whispered, "Wulfgat said it left behind so much blood, there is no way it could have lived."

I had prayed that it was true. Now Esher confirmed our greatest hope.

"The contingent has returned, my lord," he told Hrothgar. "The creature fled to its lair, where they say it has surely died. Human or animal, nothing could survive such an injury."

Hrothgar nodded at his advisor's words. Joy spread across his face until it seemed he would not be able to restrain the emotion.

"Let us go then," he said with a tremor in his voice. I gave his arm a reassuring squeeze and we made our way in anticipation to the great hall. I resisted the urge to hurry the king along, instead proceeding at a stately pace despite the quickness of my heart.

We came at length to the doors of Heorot. Oh, miracle! We stared in elation at the fiendish claw hanging high in the rafters. Esher was right—the monster could not have survived.

The king gazed with wonder on the trophy. At last he spoke, tearful and glad. "I thank the gods and goddesses for delivering us from our affliction," he said. "Life has been difficult for the Danes. Many is the time we despaired. But one warrior, with steadfast heart and steadier nerve, has changed it all with one act." He turned to Beowulf, who stood beside the door. "For what you have done for the Danish people, Lord Beowulf, you are evermore precious to me. Consider yourself as a son. Anything I have is yours to take. Glory and fame will surely be yours forever."

I gave Hrothgar a quick glance. Like a son? Surely he did not mean that Beowulf should rule the Danes. There was no doubt the Geat warrior would make a mighty king someday, but the Danish kingdom already had its heir.

Beowulf bowed in thanks for Hrothgar's words and replied, "What was done was done with the most devout dedication to the task. I wish only that the monster itself hung here instead of merely a claw. I had hoped you would be able to see it dead, the creature that inflicted so much pain upon your people."

"This is a remarkable deed," Unferth said admiringly, examining the limb. "No sword could have hacked through this

unyielding hide. There is something magical in its toughness."
Ladies murmured agreement.

After a few more moments of admiring the trophy, the people
moved off for a cheerful midday meal. When the repast was complete, Hrothgar gave the order to begin repairs to Heorot.

The damage was immense. Only the roof had escaped the
night's violence. It was a wonder the building still stood after the
clash of hero and monster.

Hundreds of hands set to the task that was now nearest the
Danes' hearts. Rebuilding and refurbishing our great hall seemed
the most joyous work we had ever undertaken. Everyone had a
job, even the little ones. They swept debris away and carted out
rubbish while we cleaned up the splintered wood and ashes, scat-
tered remnants of the monster's last attempt at domination.

In the smithy, workers forged new fastenings and bars for the
door while carpenters repaired the structure, shoring up beams and
reaffixing benches to the floor. The children gathered fresh wood
for the fire and spread clean hay on the reconstructed seats. From
quarters and storerooms, we women brought out the household
treasures, precious items of silver and gold that had been hidden
away all these years. There was much laughter and chattering as
we cleaned, arranged, and decorated.

Finally, I ordered in the tapestries, and servants carried them
carefully from the queen's quarters to the great hall. The workers
stopped to admire the gorgeous colors and well-wrought scenes as
they were hung at last on the walls. The long strips of fabric hid
some of the damage and did much to diminish evidence of the
recent destruction.

The tapestries were final proof that good fortune had returned
to Heorot. Our community's glorious history was depicted in
panel after panel—even the creature's defeat, though it was a limb

and not a head that Beowulf had actually succeeded in securing. The flowers that sprang from the drops of blood in the picture were the hopes and dreams of the Danes, a people reborn at last.

When night fell, Heorot could not be recognized as the place it had been the day before. The great hall shimmered with life and light. For the first time in a long time, we lit the lamps on the walls, and radiance shone from every newly appointed surface. Firelight flickered in the gold and silver of the household treasures, and gleamed in the warriors' weapons and ladies' jewelry. I had despaired of ever seeing it this way again.

Abundance was the hallmark of the Danes as we feasted magnificently, making generous prayers of thanks to the gods and goddesses. With toast after toast, warriors praised the king and the hero.

Jubilant, Hrothgar presented gifts to Beowulf and his men. First, he made a present to the hero of a beautifully sewn banner entwined with golden thread. Next, he gave him a sturdy helmet and a fine mail shirt. Then the king bestowed upon Beowulf an ancestral sword set with gems and plated with gold.

Finally, Hrothgar called for the stable guard, and eight horses with golden bridles were led into the hall. One of them wore a spectacular saddle of intricately jeweled design. I recognized it at once as the king's war saddle. It had served him well in many fierce battles over the years.

"Enjoy these gifts," Hrothgar told Beowulf. "I hope they will serve you as they have served me."

To the other Geat warriors the king presented valuable weaponry—treasures that would prove immensely helpful when they found themselves again in combat.

Then it was time to pass around the ceremonial cup. From the time I heard Hrothgar call Beowulf his son—though I knew it was a moment of great emotion—a suspicion had nagged my happiness. It was probably nothing, but I intended to allay my worries with a few well-chosen words of celebration.

Approaching Hrothgar, I held out the horn cup with both hands and said, "Take this cup, beloved king, and be generous to these Geats, remembering all they have done for you. There is no better use for the treasure you and your warriors have collected over the years."

Taking a breath, I continued, "I have heard you say you wish Beowulf to be as a son to you. Now that Heorot has been cleansed of evil, there is no better purpose for your treasure than to provide our Geat friends with all they deserve. But remember that your kingdom and your people belong to your children. I feel certain our dear Hrothulf will be an excellent protector for our boys should we need him. Remembering the love we have given him, I know that our nephew will provide for Hrethric and Hrothmund long after we are gone."

Hrothgar nodded and drank. Satisfied, I turned to where my boys and Hrothulf sat in the royal place of honor. Beowulf was seated between them like a member of the family. There was no doubt in my mind that he deserved honor and treasure. But the kingdom of the Danes already had its heir. Given his tranquil reaction to my speech, it seemed that my husband understood.

I passed the cup, and after another round of prayers and toasts, presented Beowulf with more gifts of thanks. I gave him armrings of twisted gold and a fine iron-ringed mail shirt. My favorite gift was one that I chose myself from the treasure stores. Fashioned of wide, heavy gold, it was a necklace set with precious stones of red and blue, and stamped with the intricate interwoven pattern of our people.

"Take this collar," I said, "and may it bring you luck, dear

Beowulf. I will thank the gods and goddesses for you every day of my life. Your goodness and your courage will surely be known throughout the world forever. I wish you happiness, and hope you will be a friend to my sons, and my people, always."

"I thank you, my lady," Beowulf said steadily as I placed the collar around his neck. "My greatest desire was to keep my promise to you. It is done, and I am satisfied." I smiled at him fondly and returned to my seat at Hrothgar's side.

Strumming his lyre, the storyteller began a song in praise of the hero. I looked then at Beowulf, who grinned like a boy as he listened to the tale. The light in his eye would ever shine on adventure, I knew it.

"Here now," the king said quietly, and I turned to him. He gazed with amusement at the advisors' bench, where to my surprise I saw that Unferth had unsheathed Hrunting and was displaying the ancient sword to Hrothmund. As our son admired the silver-encrusted hilt and ancient inlaid runes, I thought I saw the shadow of a smile on the taciturn advisor's face.

My eye fell then on Eir and Esher. In the midst of the happy, boisterous multitude, the expectant couple were managing to hold a quiet, personal conversation. I was so thankful that their babe would never know the horror our people had suffered. I could tell Esher felt the same way when the normally reserved advisor put his hand on his wife's belly and smiled into her eyes.

"This night is a wonder," I said to Hrothgar. "Can it be that we rule over a happy, peaceful people once more?"

"Indeed, my queen," he replied. "It is the happiest of days for the Danes. But something even more wonderful is about to unfold."

"What is it?" I looked at him, curious, as he stood up stiffly, giving a slight groan as he rose. Standing before me, my husband made the formal bow and held out his hand.

I laughed heartily at his stern expression. "Do you ask me to dance, my lord?"

"No, my lady," he said. "I command it."

We spun about the room, the jovial hall whirling past us in a swirl of newfound joy. I glimpsed Frea's slightly embarrassed countenance as we swung past her. It might not be dancing to her standards, but I was glad she could see it. In truth, the children hardly knew what to make of our gaiety. They had never seen such joyous celebration in all their lives.

The monster was gone, gone forever. It still seemed like a dream, to finally be rid of the horror that had tortured us for twelve long years. The future opened up like a new flower, full of beauty and potential.

We celebrated late into the darkness. At last Hrothgar and I prepared to retire, drinking one last toast to Odin the Allfather and wishing the people a good night. Weary but content, we made our way to my quarters.

Beowulf was given separate rooms specially prepared in his honor, while Danes and Geats alike lay down with satisfaction in the great hall. Heorot could once more claim ownership to what it was—the greatest meadhall in the world.

Chapter Nineteen

Ginnar was having a dream.

She and Grendel sat on benches in the meadhall of the deserted village they had found long ago. She was explaining to him the uses for the various human items around them.

"This is roasted boar, my favorite," she told him hungrily, taking the meat in her hands.

Across from her at the table, her boy wore the armor and helmet of a warrior. He held a massive silver horn cup filled with mead, from which he guzzled with great gulps.

"And here is the peppered soup your father loves," she said, pointing to a bowl on the table. "Where is he? The repast is growing cold."

Grendel said nothing but continued to drink greedily from the cup.

"You know about the horn," she said, "but this instrument is a lyre. The storyteller strums it while he sings."

Grendel cocked his head as though listening.

"And that is a drum," she continued, standing up. She realized then she wore a beautiful dress that swirled as she moved.

"The musicians play it when we dance." She spun around to demonstrate.

"Mother," he said. She smiled at him and swirled around the room as the music began to play merrily.

For some reason her boy didn't want her to dance. He slammed the horn cup down on the table and looked past her to the throneseat.

"Mother!" he shouted again. She came to a gradual halt, the dress still swirling about her feet. She turned slowly and looked at the royal dais.

Freda sat on the throne, the golden queen's circlet on her head. Her arms were covered in gleaming rings, and her crystal necklace sparkled with twinkles of light. Ginnar felt the sudden pull of the water as it surged and receded, drawing the hem of her dress with it.

Freda stared at Ginnar solemnly and spoke as though from very far away.

"You cannot fight the moon," she said. "You cannot hold him forever."

"Mother!"

Ginnar wanted to turn to her boy, to answer his cry, but she couldn't. She tried to call his name, and found she had no voice. Panic rose in her like a drowning tide.

"Mother."

Deep in hibernation, she struggled to wake. The dream faded. Sluggish and blind, she fell out of her hole and began to crawl through the tunnels toward the sound. After some moments, consciousness returned fully and she rushed past debris and rusting weapons to the main room of their lair.

"I'm coming, Grendel," she called.

She tore into the cave. Oh, nightmare!

Her boy lay bleeding his last on the murky floor. An arm was gone, and the gore oozing from his body formed a bright red cloud in the water.

She sank down beside him and took him in her arms as she had not since he was a child.

"Grendel! Grendel!" she cried. He looked at her foggily, a bemused expression on his twisted face.

She sang to him then, a song she did not know she remembered.

Drømde mig en drøm she nat,
um silki ok ærlik pæl.

I dreamt a dream last night,
of silk and fine fur.

Life flowed gently from the ragged wound. She saw that the stars were leaving her boy's eyes.

"Do you remember the wilderness, my little one?" she asked him softly. "How you used to run and play?"

He stared sightless at the ceiling.

"Where you are going," she said, "there is nothing but running and playing in the forest, and all the animals you can hunt. More creatures to catch than you have ever seen. You will be the finest hunter there."

And so her boy died.

Ginnar howled her grief with a cry that obliterated all other sensation. When she stopped, pain rushed in, tying her thoughts into anguished knots of loss and fear.

Eventually a solitary idea emerged from the chaos.

She looked around their lair at the spoils Grendel had collected over the years. Gleaming armor, swords of giants, enchanted shields—she would not need such weaponry. A lifetime of sorrow and bitterness coalesced slowly into a jagged, wieldable implement of hatred.

Vengeance. The blood price must be paid.

Ginnar sat in cheerless silence for a long time, rocking her boy gently as his body began to stiffen. When the night grew black, she lay him down tenderly and set out for the hall.

She followed the trail he had left behind him, his blood leading to the doors of the cursed hall. With a sharp stab of agony she saw her boy's arm hanging above her.

She would make them suffer.

They were deep in sleep after their revelry, and slow to react as she burst through the door. Signs of their celebration were everywhere. In a blur she saw the remains of the feast, the household treasures, the tapestries of victory and protection—and humans all around. The smell made her sick.

Sluggishness gave way to panic as they realized she had come. Clumsy and belated, some reached for their weapons and shields. She moved swiftly, snatching up a noble one and snapping its neck in an instant while it slept.

In seconds, she had fled the hall and galloped back to the mere with her warm, limp trophy and her boy's severed arm.

At the shore, she tore the head from the body and threw it to the ground. It rolled bumpily and came to rest beside a rock, staring sightless, just like her boy.

She threw the body to the creatures of the mere, who shredded it and gulped it down.

"You killed my babe," she shouted at the lifeless visage. But her ire was already fading.

She stood at the edge of the mere as the sky hinted daybreak.

The skeletal branches of the trees that lined the lake would be the last she saw of the forest. They used to love the forest, Ginnar and her boy.

Diving into fetid water with the recovered limb, she swam quickly past foul creatures who hastened to get out of her way. In the cave, Grendel lay where she had left him, armless, bloodless, dead. She roared with anguish at the sight, wounded anew by her lost boy.

After a while, she lifted him up gently and retreated to the recesses of their lair. She knew the humans would come. But she had nothing to lose now, and death would welcome them.

Taking her boy into her arms, she closed her eyes and was back in Helming, in the meadhall with her husband by her side. She could see the painted pillars, the gleaming treasures—the precious tapestries she had woven herself. Freda and their king sat on the throneseats, smiling serenely at the happy family.

Ginnar looked down fondly at the babe in her arms. "My Grendel," she said, admiring his smooth, soft skin and flawless limbs. He cooed quietly, looking out with bright eyes on the scene around him. Innocent interest shone in his sweet features.

"It is good to be born into our world," she whispered to her boy. "You'll have everything you could ever need."

Chapter Twenty

A guard shouting at the door of my quarters startled us from sleep. In a daze, I followed Hrothgar to the great hall, where we discovered the old nightmare reborn.

The warriors were in an uproar and shouted all at once.

"A monster," one cried.

"A foul creature has attacked Heorot," said another.

"It's the monster's dam!"

"A female monster."

"It has taken the advisor!"

"It has taken the trophy."

"What? What?" Hrothgar exclaimed. "Taken who?"

"Esher, my lord," a warrior replied as the group fell suddenly silent.

Hrothgar staggered against a post and I rushed to help him. "Call Lord Unferth," I told a guard.

I helped Hrothgar up the stairs of the dais and onto his throne. His expression was empty, and he breathed in rapid, shallow bursts.

.rth rushed up, slumber in his eyes. "What has happened?"
.ed the king.

Hrothgar did not speak.

"Esher has been taken by a second creature," I said shakily, when it became clear the king would not reply. "They say it is the monster's mother."

Unferth dropped heavily onto a bench and stared at Hrothgar.

After a moment, the king raised his head. The look in his eyes was terrible. I saw a desolation that frightened me.

"Send for Beowulf," he said. Unferth bowed and hurried from the hall.

I did not dare to speak as we waited for the great warrior. Stunned by Esher's disappearance, I was equally distressed by the effect on Hrothgar. Would we never be rid of tragedy? With a jolt, I realized that I must tell Eir her husband was gone. The approach of the Geat contingent saved me from dwelling on this sorrowful thought, though I knew I must face it very soon.

Beowulf and his warriors entered the great hall quickly, perplexed and alarmed at being summoned before dawn.

"Greetings, my king," Beowulf said, bowing before the throne. "How went your night? Was it as quiet as you had hoped?"

"My night?" Hrothgar exclaimed in a burst of emotion. "Do not ask me. My beloved Esher is gone—my closest companion on the battlefield when we were young warriors with a kingdom to build. There was no better man for war, or for peace. And now he has been taken by the monster's dam. She breached our hall and made off with him before anyone could act. He would have given all for his people, and now he is lost."

The king's voice shook with grief. The hall was silent as he sunk back into the throneseat. After a moment he sat up wearily and spoke again.

"There is a lake, the creature's lair. It will have returned there."

Beowulf glanced at me.

"I have heard of this unfortunate mere," he said.

"I was there, twelve years ago," Hrothgar heaved. "It was foul, and bubbled with blood. A black mist shrouded the grisly creatures who swam there."

The king gazed at the far wall, peering into the past. "A band of my best warriors and I set out that day," he said, "to destroy the creature that dared offend Heorot. Only I returned. For twelve long years, we suffered its terrible oppression—until you arrived, Lord Beowulf, and killed it."

Looking the Geat leader in the eye, Hrothgar said, "Now we turn to you for help once more. If you have the courage, get yourself to that awful place and kill the monster's dam. If you return to us, we will repay you as gratefully as before, with treasure and Danish gold."

Beowulf regarded the despondent king and said gently, "My lord. Let us not dwell on the grief of this great loss."

He put his hand on the hilt of his sword. "It is better to avenge death than to mourn it. Life ends for all of us, but our fame lives on. Come, my lord, let us ride together to this lake, where we will kill the monster's dam. I promise you she will find no respite from me."

My mouth agape, I stared horrified at Beowulf, then at Hrothgar as he reacted to the bold words.

Sitting up suddenly, the king leaned forward, intrigued by the suggested venture.

No, no! I thought to myself, clenching my fists as I fought to remain silent.

Hrothgar glanced at me and then at Beowulf. "We will go," he said firmly. "Prepare the horses. We ride at dawn."

I lagged behind as the king left the hall. I hoped to speak to Beowulf, and watched him as the warriors dispersed to prepare for battle. The Geat leader noticed my gaze and came to me at once.

"My lady," he said, bowing.

"The king is old," I said furtively. "He is old, Lord Beowulf, and he should not go with you."

"My lady," he replied, "Hrothgar has lost his best advisor—his dearest battle companion. Only retribution can ease his grief."

"And what of my grief should he not return? What of the people, who have lost their best advisor? Should they now lose their king?"

To my astonishment, the Geat warrior smiled.

"Hrothgar is fortunate to have a queen who cares for him as you do," he said. "You can be counted on to do what is best for him."

I scoured his young face angrily. In the steady eyes and resolute jaw, I saw Hrothgar as he had been long ago. There was a grim determination in the Geat leader's countenance, and—though I did not want to hear it—a warrior's wisdom in his words.

I sighed and bowed my head in resignation. "So be it."

As the sun rose, Hrothgar and Beowulf set out for the lake, accompanied by the Geat warriors and a contingent of Danes. Lord Unferth and I saw them off at the edge of the village.

"Lord Beowulf," Unferth said as they mounted their battle horses. "I offer you Hrunting, my sword." Unsheathing the shining blade, he presented it humbly to the Geat leader. "It has an honorable history. I pray it serves you well."

Beowulf reached down and took the silver hilt in his steady grip. He held the gleaming sword up to the light. "I thank you, Lord Unferth," he said. "Hrunting is a fine weapon, and if wyrd permits, it will be the death of the monster's dam."

I stepped up to Hrothgar on his mount and unwillingly found myself back at that morning twelve years before, when he had embarked upon a similar journey.

"May victory be yours," I repeated the traditional battle prayer. "And may you return to me safely, my king, in triumph over the killer." My husband raised his hand in salute and turned toward the forest.

I watched them ride away with sunken heart. The warriors' terrible task was underway, and I had my own dreadful duty to fulfill.

"Fetch Lady Muni," I instructed a servant and made my way to my quarters.

When Muni arrived, I sat down with her, and said, "Muni, you must be strong for me."

"What is it?" she asked, worried.

"Esher has been seized by the monster's dam," I told her, explaining the inconceivable situation. As tears fell, I knew my friend was thinking of Wigmund, her first husband, who had been taken from her in just the same way.

"We must go to Eir now," I said. "The sun is up, and she will be rising."

The children were still sleeping in the adjoining room when a servant led us into the healer's quarters. Eir stood slowly with a smile, then, seeing our faces, immediately grew somber.

"What is it?" she asked.

There was no way to soften the news. "Eir," I said as steadily as I could, "a terrible thing has happened. The monster had a dam, and it came to the hall sometime before sunrise, and it took Esher."

It was horrible to watch the pain make its way across her face—that wrenching transformation from cheer to disbelief to anguish. Muni moved quickly to her side as Eir put a hand on her belly and sank to a bench.

"He is gone?" she said.

"Yes. Hrothgar and Beowulf and their warriors have ridden to the mere."

"They will not find him alive," she said dully.

"Eir," Muni said tearfully. "I'm so sorry."

Eir looked at her. "Gone," she said, beginning to cry.

I put my arms around my friends and we wept.

In the next room, the children began to stir. "The girls are waking," I said, sniffing. "Do you want me to see to them?"

Eir stifled a sob and struggled to stand up. "No," she replied. "I must tell them. They will know something is wrong. There is no sense in delay."

We watched as she moved slowly into the other room.

Muni and I looked at each other and she took my hand. "Will you stay with her?" I asked, gripping hers tight. "You know what she feels."

Muni nodded unhappily.

"I must see to the weaving sheds, and then to the kitchens," I said, standing up. "I will take care of those things, and you take care of Eir."

I spent the morning tending to chores, grateful for even the slightest respite from thinking on our tragedy—and from wondering whether my husband would return alive.

On my way from kitchen to hall, I stood before the great doors and gazed up to the rafters where the monster's limb had been.

How was it that we could go from horror to happiness to horror again so quickly? Hadn't our people suffered enough?

It came time to prepare the evening repast, and my worry increased. The retinue had now been gone so long that the fretful doubt of their return loomed intolerably in my thoughts. What was the point of preparing the meal if they were not going to return? But no. I shook my head. It must be done.

As the hour of the repast drew near, I heard at last the announcement I had been waiting for.

"The king approaches," a guard cried.

I ran outside to the ring of gathering as the horses thundered up to the hall. At the head of the retinue, Hrothgar appeared uninjured, though weary. I realized as I looked over the group that neither Beowulf nor any of the other Geats was present.

Hrothgar dismounted and took my hand.

"You came back to me," I said. He nodded without speaking and we made for his quarters in silence.

Inside, as I helped him take off his armor and battle dress, I asked cautiously, "Where is Beowulf?"

Hrothgar threw himself down onto the bed and sighed with unhappiness.

"He went into the lake," he said, "but he didn't come out."

I sat down beside my husband as he told the dismal tale.

They had ridden hard for the mere, slowing to a cautious trot when they entered the ancient forest that surrounded it.

"The lake remains as it was all those years ago," Hrothgar said, describing its blood-stained surface and murky waves. "Our eyes were fixed on the foul creatures in the putrid water—so many of them, writhing and snapping at one another—when suddenly a warrior cried, 'Look!'"

The king's voice broke. "It was Esher's head, lying sightless on the shore."

I gasped in grief as he spoke the painful words. I had hoped somehow the advisor might still be alive.

Hrothgar continued, "Then one of the water creatures skirted the shore, and Beowulf skewered it. I think it must have heartened him, for he at once determined to enter the water to seek out the monster's lair.

"We waited long hours by that poisonous lake, hoping in vain that he would reappear. Finally, with a rush of sound there came a great eruption of bubbling blood and gore to the surface—but no Beowulf."

The king sighed. "I decided then to return to Heorot. It is almost certain that he is dead, may the gods and goddesses bless him. His fellow Geats would not come with us, however, and remain at the lake. If they linger when night falls, I doubt any will survive."

Desolation seeped into my heart as I considered Beowulf's death. This was the cruelty of wyrd, that we should have hope so briefly, and lose it so unexpectedly. What was worse, our beloved Esher was gone.

"What now?" I lamented. "Our nightmare begins anew? Another creature comes to torment us? No hero to save us?"

"No Esher," Hrothgar said dimly.

All our joy an illusion, I thought.

Mustering what little resolve remained to us, we made our way to the hall for the evening meal. Gloom had fallen once again over the people, and there was little talking. We had thought ourselves free, but instead, we were broken.

Chapter Twenty-one

"Try to eat something, my lord," I begged Hrothgar as he sat listlessly on his throne.

"I am not hungry," he replied. I sighed as a servant refilled our cups. I had no appetite either. Eating hardly seemed worth the effort.

I paused with the mead cup to my lips, attention captured by a commotion at the doors of the hall. Murmurs became shouts as a contingent of warriors tramped into the main room. Weary and remarkable, they boldly approached the dais. Beowulf!

We gaped at the hero and his men as they came to a halt before us, placing their heavy burden at our feet. Beowulf put a hand on his trophy—the massive, staring head of the monster.

Reality abruptly became unreal. Everything I thought I knew about my future—the hardship, the hopelessness—melted away in an instant, replaced by the most extraordinary optimism. Like a corpse that suddenly begins to breathe, my living was a miracle.

The same feeling shone in the faces of the people as they spied the hideous head. "Hurrah! Hurrah!" they shouted, leaping from their seats and embracing one another. Hrothgar and I bounded to our feet with newfound energy.

"Beowulf!" Hrothgar exclaimed. "Your return is a gift beyond any I had hoped for. I see that you bring us the best of news."

"Greetings, good king," the warrior replied. "I bring you valuable spoils of battle, the rewards of a hard fight beneath the surface of the gloomy lake."

I gazed at the monstrous head in disgust and delight as Beowulf told his heroic tale.

"When I left dry land to seek the monster's lair," he began, "I plunged through filth till I thought my lungs would burst. Just when I had determined to return to the surface, the monster's dam appeared and grabbed me. As she dragged me through the water, lesser creatures swarmed about us, eager for fresh meat. I found myself then in a cave, where pockets of air allowed me to breathe while the monster's dam tried to kill me.

"I swung at her then with Hrunting, a mighty blow with that good sword that would have sundered the helmet of a warrior and sliced his skull. The sword merely glanced off the creature's hide. I resolved then to subdue her with my bare hands, as I had her monstrous son. I lay hold of her shoulder and threw her to the ground. But at that moment the cursed mother had the better of me, leaping up and rushing forward, all frightful claw and fang. She wrestled me down and jabbed at my chest with her daggers till only well-wrought chain mail stood between me and death. I rolled away, gasping and battered. As I scrambled to avoid the next lunge, my eyes fell on a giant's sword—one of countless treasures that lay in heaps about the cave. It was too large to be wielded by an average man, but I rose to my feet and gripped it firmly. Raging and desperate for my life, I swung with fury, slicing through the creature's neck in one swift blow.

"The monster's dam fell dead to the floor. At once I searched and found what I was seeking. The powerful sword sang again, decapitating the lifeless body of her cursed son. The tainted blood was so vile and poisonous that the blade of the giant's sword melted instantly, leaving nothing but the gold-encrusted hilt.

"I left all the hoarded plunder, returning to the surface with only the hilt of the sword and the monster's head. My warriors had supposed me dead, and were overjoyed when I rose from the water.

"Now here we are, and here is the prize you have longed for, my lord. I add to it the golden hilt. You are free at last from your oppression."

Beowulf presented the hilt to Hrothgar, who took it in both hands. He turned it over, carefully examining the inlaid runes and jeweled design.

The great hall fell silent as the king began to speak.

"I have ruled the Danes for a lifetime," he said, "and I know that here is the better man."

He looked at the hero. "My dear Beowulf, all the world speaks of your fame, yet you wield your power sensibly and with grace. Our vow of friendship remains strong. I know that you will be a good friend and go on to serve your people well.

"In this, you are most unlike the unfortunate King Heremod," Hrothgar mused thoughtfully. "That killer king became obsessed with his own greatness and ceased to be a good leader to the Danes."

"My lord," I said quietly, leaning toward my husband. "These brave warriors must be hungry and fatigued."

"Of course," he replied, standing and raising his arm into the air. "Faithful friends to the Danish kingdom," he said, "we thank you. Take your ease and feast with us. Let us celebrate this great victory with sustenance and song."

At his words, the musicians scurried to their instruments and struck up a jubilant refrain. Servants brought forth fresh platters of meat and bread while the Geats washed off their grime and took the places of honor. When the mead had been poured and the repast was underway, Hrothgar turned to the great warrior and said, "With age such as mine comes wisdom, Lord Beowulf, and I hope that you will listen to what I tell you now.

"There is that fortunate chieftain who has all that he could hope for: a great hall, a strong army, a wide kingdom. He wants for nothing, suffers no illness or misfortune, and the world leaps up at his command.

"But he becomes arrogant in his well-being, and his conscience slumbers deep in a bed of conceit. Thus is he unprepared for the evil that sneaks up on him. Self-indulgence overtakes wisdom, and the ruler no longer gives gifts to his warriors, but instead hoards his treasure and alienates the people. When he dies, he dies alone. A new lord comes along and distributes the hoarded wealth.

"But let it not be so with you, Lord Beowulf. Today you are young and strong, a mighty warrior with none to oppose you. Someday, however, whether it be by sickness or by sword, by fire or by flood, by spear or by old age, death will come. It comes to us all.

"I have ruled the Danes for a lifetime, and once thought my successes so complete that no enemy could oppose me. Then the monster came and killed our people, terrorizing the nation for twelve long years. I thank the gods and goddesses that I have lived to see this day, when the killer's head rests here in our long-ravaged hall, and peace has come to us at last."

Hrothgar held his cup out to Beowulf. "A toast to you and your warriors," he said. "Gifts will be yours when we rise in the morning."

"I thank you, my lord," Beowulf replied.

"The Allfather was with us today," Hrothulf exclaimed as the cup went round.

"It is believed," Unferth spoke up suddenly, "that these monsters were sent by dark gods to torment the Danes. That they were evil creatures brought up from the underworld who could not tolerate the people's goodness and chose to crush it. I thank the gods that we finally have our vengeance on these cursed beasts."

Before I even knew that I intended to speak, I heard myself say, "Surely, Lord Unferth, if there is one thing we have learned, it is that steadfast faith, not hostile arrogance, more wisely guides us in times of trial."

Unferth scowled but could not reply, for the crowd began to cheer as the guards approached the creature's great head. Grunting and staggering under its weight, they carried the gory trophy outside to stake it for display in front of Heorot—a reminder that our days of terror were ended.

Chapter Twenty-two

The next morning dawned clear and bright, a new life for the Danish people. Like all battle-weary warriors, Beowulf and his contingent were eager to return home. Elated with our freedom but saddened by their leaving, we gathered in the great hall for the ceremonies of parting.

Unferth sat beside Muni's husband Wulfgar on the advisors' bench, and I noticed that Hrothgar never once looked at them during the rituals. It must hurt too badly to see that Esher was not there.

Beowulf approached Unferth with the sword Hrunting in his hands.

"Lord Unferth," he said, "I return this ancestral sword to your care. Hrunting is a fine weapon, and I thank you for its use."

Unferth accepted the sword quietly. I saw with surprise that his expression was one of humility rather than scorn. It was plain Beowulf's triumph and Esher's death had affected the proud advisor. I reflected that even those we think unalterable can still be transformed by life's events.

Beowulf came then to the throne and bowed to the king. "King

Hrothgar," he said, "I thank you for your hospitality. We Geats have been well engaged in your hall. But we yearn for our home, and sail today for Geatland.

"If the king of the Danes ever again has need of me," he continued, "I will return. Any enemy who dares to menace you as the monster did will have to deal with the Geats. I know King Hygelac shares my view of this friendship. And should your son, young Hrethric, ever desire to visit the hall of the Geats, he will find himself among friends there. Foreign lands offer much to the warrior who is worthy to receive their gifts."

Moved by the hero's oath of friendship, Hrothgar said, "Odin the Allfather must have sent you those words, my dear Beowulf. I have never heard a warrior so young speak with such insight. Truly, the more I know you, the more I like you. You are strong in body, robust in mind, and powerful in speech. You will make a fine king someday."

Hrothgar raised his arm, and a servant hurried forward to place an ornate wooden box upon the dais.

The king of the Danes stood and said, "Accept this gift of precious ornaments crafted by our finest metalworkers. Let this treasure be a reminder to you of the lasting peace between us. Wars and feuds between the Danes and the Geats are a thing of the past. Visitors from your land to mine will find warm welcome and gifts of friendship here."

Stepping down off the dais, the king embraced Beowulf warmly. "I wish you a safe, happy journey," he said, "and beg you to return to us someday."

I knew my husband hurt to tell the hero good-bye. There were tears in his voice as he said, "Farewell, my son. Though I fear we will never meet again, you will always be in my heart, and in the hearts of my people."

Beowulf returned the embrace and replied steadily, "May the gods and goddesses be with you, my lord."

And so the Geats left us. The Danish people cheered a grateful farewell as the mighty contingent strode from the hall. We shouted prayers and words of gratitude for the hero who had rescued us from our misery.

A short while later, I came to Frea in our quarters. "Walk with me," I said. She put down her weaving and followed me out of the village and across the sandy dunes.

I made my way quickly toward the beach, where I knew the Geats would be loading their ship. As we drew near, we could see the warriors urging their new horses on board and hauling up the chests full of armor and treasure.

"Queen Wealtheow approaches," called the guard.

Leaving the ship, Beowulf came toward us with a smile. "My lady," he said to me, and with a nod to Frea, "Princess."

"I come to wish you luck on your sea voyage," I told him, drawing a small square of tapestry out of the bag at my waist.

He took the delicate weaving into his strong hands, examining its minute design with care. Just a few inches across, it showed a spiral of tiny white flowers into which I had woven a spell of protection. They were the same flowers I had created in the larger tapestry, blooming where the creature's blood fell—the hopes and dreams of our people springing to life at the hero's triumph.

"I thank you, my lady," he said. "It is beautiful."

"All the treasure in the world cannot repay what you have given us," I said.

Beowulf glanced at Frea. "The Danes are blessed to have such a wise queen," he replied carefully. "I suspect they owe her more than they know."

Frea looked at me with mild curiosity.

A warrior approached the Geat leader with a bow. "The ship is loaded, my lord," he said. "We are ready to embark."

Beowulf nodded. To me, he said, "Farewell, my lady. May the gods and goddesses be with you."

"I will thank them for you daily," I replied.

He bowed and turned toward his ship.

We watched as the Geats sailed away. The curved prow of their vessel cut proudly through the waves, leaving a foaming path in its wake. We stood there a long time, sun glinting on the water, light twinkling in the waves, until the ship was just another sparkle on the sea.

"I will sail away in just such a ship," Frea said earnestly.

"To new adventures, like Beowulf," I told her. "And I will follow you with my heart."

She took my arm and we returned to Heorot in thoughtful silence.

That night, as I lay down to rest, it seemed the first time in a lifetime that I might sleep without fear of waking to tragedy.

"Here now, Wealtheow," Hrothgar said as he came to bed. "Will you make no room for an old man?"

"She who enters first, is first, my lord," I answered sweetly. He grumbled and put out the lamp at our bedside.

We lay in the dark for a few peaceful moments. Then Hrothgar said, "It is over, isn't it? The monster's domination has ended at last."

"Yes," I said. "Our children will have a better life now. And so will we." My hand found his beneath the covers. Just as I wished it for our babes, I was hopeful my husband might spend his remaining years in peace. He had suffered much, and deserved this happiness.

He squeezed my hand and said, "Esher has gone to Valhalla. I know it is the way of things, but I miss him."

"So do I," I whispered.

The loss of Hrothgar's beloved advisor hung heavy on us all, though none suffered as much as Eir. With their child due in a moon, she spent most of her time sitting and staring at nothing, hands on her belly. She had never been one to ramble, but now she barely spoke. The other women of Heorot assumed care for the three girls so that their mother could mend.

Muni and I tried to help, engaging our friend in the activities she had always loved. From discussions of weaving patterns to searches for herbs in the forest, she let us guide her without protest. Yet nothing seemed truly to matter to her, though she did well enough with the children, and made motions of taking interest.

"Only time will mend," Muni said, but my worry persisted. I felt I could see right through the crack where Eir's heart should be. It was empty, and I knew it should be full—even if sorrow and pain were its only content.

On the day of the great celebration, I decided I would wait no longer. "Eir," I said firmly, sitting down beside her in the great hall. "We must talk."

She looked at me patiently. "Yes?"

I took a breath and began the speech I had been practicing. "You have been a good friend to me," I said. "When I first arrived in the kingdom of the Danes, you comforted and guided me. You eased my sadness at having to leave my home. And through all the years of my life here, you have ever been beside me in time of trial."

Eir's eyes were filling with tears. Leaning toward her, I said, "Let me be the friend that you have been to me. Tell me what is in your heart."

Bowing her head, my friend stared at the clenched hands in

her lap. She seemed unable to speak. But then she raised head, tears on cheeks, and said, "My babe will have no fathe Wealtheow. How will it be named? If it is the boy we were hoping for, who will guide him through this life? Who will teach him to be the warrior his father was?" She began to cry.

I put my arms around her. "You need never worry for your babe. I assure you that Hrothgar will name your child, and be as a father to your son. We will help you in every way we can, I promise."

She sniffed, reassured.

"Will you come with me to the ring?" I asked gently. "It is almost time for the ceremony." She nodded, wiping her face with her sleeve. I helped her up and we made our way outside, where the people were beginning to gather in anticipation.

The moon was full again, and it was time for the bonfire. As was the way of our people, we would burn the monster's head in triumph, celebrating its defeat with jubilation.

Hrothgar and I sat on our thrones on a platform to one side of the fire while the head was removed from its stake and brought before us.

"This is a great day," said the king, raising his arm into the air. "The monster has been vanquished. Let the fire burn away our suffering, and may we rise a new, stronger people. To the Danish kingdom!"

"To the Danish kingdom!" the people cried, as guards lifted the head up and hoisted it heavily into the fire. Sparks shot into the sky and flames rushed to consume the monstrous trophy. A song of victory rose in the air.

One of the guards reached down and plucked a soiled cloth from the ground. "Wait," I called out as he moved to throw it into the flames. Hrothgar looked at me, surprised.

What is that fabric there?" I asked.

The guard looked down and replied, "It came from the creature's lair, my lady. Lord Beowulf used it to avoid touching the
monster's poisonous blood."

"It must be charmed," Hrothgar murmured. I nodded, then
frowned, gazing for a moment at the worn rag.

"Bring it to me," I said. The king nodded, and the guard
placed it on the dais.

The Danes began to dance the spiral dance, a symbol of the
wheel's endless turning and the people's constant spirit. As we
watched the ever narrowing circle close in upon itself, Hrothgar
asked, "What interests you about that cloth?"

"There is magic in the weaving," I mused. "It is familiar."
Moving to the edge of the platform, I reached down and fingered
the filthy fabric.

"Put it in a washpot," I instructed a servant, "and take it to my
quarters to soak."

My first thought when I woke in the morning was of the cloth.
I quickly gathered the necessary supplies and carried the washpot
to a secluded area behind my quarters. I poured out the old water
and filled the pot anew. Most of the soil had been removed by the
soaking. Pushing back the sleeves of my underdress, I began to
gently scrub the stains from the aged fabric.

I emptied the washpot and refilled it twice more before most
of the cloth was clean. Rinsing it in fresh water, I squeezed out the
excess and then spread the rag on a board.

The colors were faded, but the pattern of the weaving was
now quite plain. I peered at it, tracing the intricate design with
my fingertips. There was a glimmer of spell, a hopeful longing for
the future woven into the threads. Yes, there was definitely magic
in the weaving.

And there was something familiar about those threads, that pattern. Where did this cloth come from? Was it a remnant of some poor victim's cloak from the bottom of the lake? Given the style of its weaving, it might have been a blanket, though it was far too small.

This material had been exposed to the elements for a very long time. I wasn't even certain of its true color, though there was some faded red, and what might have been blue. What was it this reminded me of? The well-wrought stitches, the intricate pattern, the red and blue . . .

I sat back suddenly on my heels.

The girdle. The weaving was the same as my mother's girdle. But how?

Ginnar made this fabric. The pattern and technique were identical to that of the girdle. But how did a cloth created by the outcast companion of my mother in Helming come to be here with the monster?

The monster.

Ginnar ran to the forest with her deformed babe. Ginnar wove this fabric—a blanket for her child. Ginnar, the monster's mother. And the monster was the babe my mother and father could not save.

Astounded, I ran to find Muni. "I must talk to you," I whispered frantically when I found her in the kitchen. She nodded, curious, and hurried after me to my quarters.

"What is it?" she asked as soon as we were inside.

"You will not believe it!" I exclaimed.

"What?" Now she was excited, too.

I held the damp cloth up before her eyes.

"A rag?" she asked doubtfully. "What is that?"

"Beowulf brought it from the monster's lair," I said. "Look at the weaving."

Reluctant to touch it, she leaned over and examined the stitches closely. "The work of a gifted weaver," she said admiringly. "It must come from the cloak of a nobleman the monster killed—horrible! But in truth it seems more a blanket."

"It is a blanket," I said, working hard to tell a good story, though by this time I was fairly bursting with my extraordinary discovery. "A babe's blanket. Does the pattern remind you of anything?"

"A babe's blanket?" she said. "How do you know? No, I've never seen this pattern. Why would it remind me of anything?"

I savored the moment. "It reminds me of something," I said. Walking over to my clothes chest, I reached down past dresses and underdresses till my fingers found what they were searching for. I drew the girdle out, stretched it between my hands, and turned to her much as I had fifteen years before.

"The girdle?" Muni asked, confused.

"The girdle and this cloth—fabric found in the monster's lair—were woven by the same person," I said. "The Lady Ginnar."

"But—why—what do you mean? How could both be—" The effect was everything I expected. Muni gasped suddenly, and her eyes grew wide with astonishment. "No!" she said.

"Yes!" I exclaimed. "The monster. The monster and its mother. The monster is the babe who was cast out."

Her mouth hung open and she stared at me, speechless.

"Wyrd has wound around us in a spiral dance," I said fervently. "Here we are in the center, with two pieces of weaving creating a tapestry we could never have imagined."

"You must tell Hrothgar," she said.

"Why?" I asked. "I have pondered it. He does not even know about the girdle. What would it gain us to tell him now?" I knew

186

I ran back inside to tell Hrothgar. As he rose to dress, I threw on my clothes and hurried to Eir's quarters.

It was obvious that the babe would be born now. Having had three already, Eir knew that it would be soon.

"It will not live," she cried between the pains. I reassured her, though I suspected she was right.

An hour later the babe came, almost too weak to cry.

"It's a boy," I said as I placed it gently on the small, brightly colored blanket Eir had used with all her children. The babe uttered a faint wail, and I saw that its skin was tinged with blue. With relief I noted that despite its frailty, it was not deformed. Still, it did not appear to be long for the world.

"The king will not accept it," Muni whispered.

Eir looked at me, exhausted and heartbroken. "This is all I have of Esher," she said.

I went to the door to notify the servant, and a moment later Hrothgar entered. Walking over to the babe, he gazed down sadly at its frail form and bluish skin.

"It will not live," he said.

Eir said nothing, but looked at me pleadingly.

"Hrothgar," I said. "It might live."

He shook his head and glanced at me grimly.

"It is all I have, all I have of Esher," Eir cried, unable to control herself.

Hrothgar did not reply or look at her. I saw that he was about to declare.

"Wait," I said. I drew close and spoke quietly so that only my husband could hear. "There is something I should have told you long ago," I said. "We have good cause to let this babe live. Its life is wrapped up in the affliction we have suffered at the hands of the monster."

He looked at me, perplexed.

"The story I have to tell you will make it clear," I told him, "but at this moment, I am asking you to trust me."

The king appeared doubtful. "It is bad luck to let such a child live."

"I would not seek to bring misfortune on our people," I said urgently. "From the moment I became your queen, Hrothgar, your wyrd and mine have been one. For the sake of that joined fate, I beseech you to let wyrd decide what becomes of this child."

He frowned thoughtfully, and I said, "It is not the usual way of the people, but as king you have this right. I beg of you, let it live."

Eir and Muni were silent as the babe continued to utter its faint cry.

Hrothgar looked at me for a long moment, then bent down to pick up the weakly wailing babe. "I declare this child—" he looked at Eir.

"Esher," she said joyfully. "For his father."

"I declare this child Esher, son of Esher and Eir, nobleman of the Danes."

And so we were redeemed.

Hrothgar handed the babe to me. "Sweet babe," I cooed, putting him in his mother's arms. She cried with relief. Muni sat down next to her and covered the babe with the blanket.

I looked at Hrothgar. "Thank you," I said quietly.

"You will tell me what it means," he replied, displeased.

I bowed my head. "Yes, my lord." He nodded and left the room.

I turned to Eir and the babe. It was attempting to nurse, but was too weak to latch on.

"If little Esher does not nurse soon, we will draw the milk and use a cloth until he is strong enough," I said. "Muni did that with Ingrid, you remember." Eir nodded gratefully and Muni smiled at me.

The sun was rising when I returned to my quarters. Hrothgar sat beside the loom, fingering the beginnings of a tapestry I had fashioned there. I crossed the room and knelt before him.

"I thank the gods and goddesses for you," I said humbly.

"You have a story to tell me," he demanded, though his eyes crinkled a bit. I put my arms around him and closed my eyes.

How would I tell it? What should I say? That the great wheel of life does not always have to mean death?

I sat back and looked at my husband. He was a good man, and a good king, and he had ruled his people well for a lifetime.

Yet there are tales that must be told so we do not repeat them.

Rising resolutely, I lifted my arms into the air, as I had seen the royal storyteller do so many times.

"Hear my tale, O gods," I said, "and bless the telling."

EPILOGUE

I traversed the shore of the ancient mere, a bouquet of white flowers in my hand. They bloomed everywhere, these bright harbingers of summer. Their blossoms reminded me of the flowers that now grew in all my tapestries.

The depths of the mere were clear and clean again, and the sparkling surface rippled in the wind. Though the terrifying images were fixed forever in my mind, I still found it hard to believe that such a beautiful place could have harbored such darkness.

I came here often now that the lake had regained its purity, thinking about my mother's best childhood friend. What had she been like before she was cast out? Was she friendly and strong-willed like Muni? Or quiet and earnest like Eir? How had she changed from bright, spirited, and beautiful to terrible and cruel?

We create our own monsters.

If only this lake could have helped her as it had helped me. As it had restored the Danes for generations. As it continued to heal the people now.

I looked over to the rocky ledge that jutted from the forest at the water's edge. Eir sat cross-legged on its sun-warmed surface, eyes closed and face held to the light. In her arms, little Esher slept the peaceful slumber of a newborn babe.

It was his first journey here to this place of healing. Still weak and small—but alive—he had been brought to the ancient mere as soon as Eir believed he could travel. It was clear her babe's life would be a struggle, and he needed more than his mother's love to survive.

I walked toward them thoughtfully, pondering the flowers in my hands.

"I have sand in my shoes," Muni complained from down the shore.

"Take them off," I called, watching in amusement as she bent down to unwrap the unwieldy leather, her own hands full of the white blossoms.

"Here now," she said suddenly. "What's this?" Tossing the flowers into the water and reaching beneath the glimmering surface, Muni pulled up a square of worn, warped wood.

"What is it?" I called, peering at her from the ledge.

She moved toward us slowly, shaking the weeds from the object as she walked.

"The lake has given you a gift," Eir said.

"It has been in the water a long time," Muni noted, holding it out to us.

"A loom!" I exclaimed. "It's a handloom."

Eir shuddered. "Another spoil from the vile fiend's lair."

I didn't think so. Monster or no, something told me that Ginnar had not relinquished every vestige of her humanity. "Let's talk over here," I said to Muni, "lest we wake the babe."

"You have been shouting right next to the babe," Muni protested. Catching my eye, she said, "Oh," and followed me out of Eir's hearing.

"What is it?" she asked, curious.

"I believe this belonged to Ginnar," I replied. "I did not want to mention it in front of Eir. It is difficult to have sympathy for the killer of your husband."

Muni nodded. "Shall we throw it back in?"

"No," I said firmly. "I will keep it. Eir was right. The lake has given it to us. It is the tool of a gifted weaver, though her skills were twisted and used for evil. We will take this offering, and use it for good. I will weave a gift for Eir's babe, and imbue it with spells of strength and protection to help little Esher grow strong."

Muni nodded again thoughtfully, and we made our way back to where Eir sat nursing her babe. She hummed a sweet song as he drank, and I recognized with a start the lullaby my mother had taught Muni. I never sang it to my babes, because it reminded me too much of my first lost one.

"How do you know that song?" I asked. "Did Muni teach it to you?"

Eir looked up at me, surprised. "I don't know," she said. "The tune just came into my head."

The three of us began to hum the lovely melody. Gazing contentedly on the tranquil scene, I leaned against the trunk of one of the gnarled trees whose roots grew down into the mere.

Abruptly, a long-forgotten sensation flooded through me. I could feel it! The life that grew beneath the bark—I could feel it. And it was just like mine. We were one again. Grateful and happy, I said a silent prayer for the tree spirit, and felt its blessing in return.

"You must instruct me on the words to that song," I said then to Muni. "I would teach it to Frea before she goes." I tossed my flowers into the mere, and we watched the breeze bear them away across the water.